"Then let me continue to be forthcoming with the truth for your own good," Alice said. "How much do you know about Byron Gates?"

"Not much," Vera admitted. "Only that he's charming and handsome. Quite pleasant, really."

"Of course he is. He's a carefree bachelor. No doubt he uses smooth words to captivate all the ladies. And that is why, my dear sister, he is not a suitable match for you," Alice cautioned. "I advise you to stay away from Byron, and I expect you to heed that advice."

"How do you know so much about him?"

"After you mentioned him to me on the evening of the social, I had Elmer do some digging for me."

"Alice! You certainly didn't waste any time. Why are you worried? I don't even know Byron. At least not very well." Vera tore out the stitch she had just crocheted.

"True, but you have never expressed interest in any man before now."

"That's just what Katherine said," Vera noted.

"And she is a lifelong friend of yours. So you can see why I believe that my fears are not unfounded."

"Fears?"

"Yes." Alice sighed, a sad look reaching into her eyes. "I'm afraid I don't like what Elmer told me about your Mr. Gates."

"What did he discover?"

"Byron Gates is a known rake, cad, and gambler. No honest woman in Baltimore will have him, and neither should you. I recommend strongly that you stay away from him. And Elmer agrees."

TAMELA HANCOCK MURRAY is an award-winning, best-selling author living in Northern Virginia. She and her husband of over twenty years are blessed with two daughters. Their first, an honors student, is a college freshman at Tamela's alma mater. Their second, a student at Christian school, keeps them busy with church activities and AWANA. Tamela loves to take mini vacations with her family, and she also enjoys reading and Bible study.

Books by Tamela Hancock Murray

Vera's Turn for Love

Tamela Hancock Murray

Blessings and peace,
Tamela

Heartsong Presents

With love to Carrie, Kathie, Sally, and Vickie

A note from the Author:
*I love to hear from my readers! You may correspond with
me by writing:*

Tamela Hancock Murray
Author Relations
PO Box 721
Uhrichsville, OH 44683

ISBN 1-59789-061-8

VERA'S TURN FOR LOVE

All scripture quotations are taken from the King James Version of the
Bible.

All of the characters and events in this book are fictitious. Any resem-
blance to actual persons, living or dead, or to actual events is purely
coincidental.

*Our mission is to publish and distribute inspirational products offering
exceptional value and biblical encouragement to the masses.*

PRINTED IN THE U.S.A.

one

Near Hagerstown, Maryland, 1902

"Who is that man?" Vera Howard whispered in Katherine Bagley's ear.

The church social hummed with voices, but Vera didn't want to eye the new man too closely. Trying to conceal her interest, she cast her gaze over other parts of the social hall. A picture of Jesus as a child hung in one corner by an arched window. A few feet away, little girls tried to outperform one another on the upright piano. She watched one group of friends after another as they talked—anything to keep from setting her stare on the irresistible stranger. No need to let the object of her curiosity, with his wavy black hair, flashing blue eyes, and fine form, suspect he had attracted her interest. True, the twentieth century had dawned, but discretion never went out of fashion.

"You want to know about that man?" Katherine's mouth slackened, and her brown eyes grew wide. "Vera! I've never heard you ask such a question!"

Heat rose to Vera's cheeks, yet she couldn't resist taking a second peek at the dark-haired stranger. At that moment, he laughed with a gusto that showed his enjoyment of the conversation. She liked a man who could laugh without inhibition. Who wouldn't be drawn to such vitality and comeliness? Suddenly fearful of swooning, she took a seat, being careful not to let any punch spill on her cream-colored dress. "I don't suppose I should have asked."

Katherine sat beside her and nudged her in the ribs. "No, of course you should if you want to know. It's just that you shocked me because you've never asked about a gentleman before this moment. Tell you what. Let me see what I can discover for you." She finished her punch, set down the cup, and rose to fulfill her promise before Vera could object.

Katherine was right. Vera had never been especially intrigued by any new man at church. Of course, men she didn't know joined their church or just visited from time to time—comely men at that. But they were usually accompanied by a pretty wife and several young children. This man appeared to be alone.

She eyed Ethel, who was known to be seeking a suitor. No doubt Ethel would bat her long black eyelashes at him all too soon. Vera, with a slight frame and face she thought pleasant enough but not beautiful, decided that she didn't stand a chance against such a bold and coy rival. Withholding a sigh, Vera fanned herself against heat that seemed to increase as the crowd grew more animated. Or was she hot with emotion?

Katherine returned and sat in the empty seat beside Vera. The brunette leaned toward Vera. "I found out who your mystery man is." Katherine's eyes glowed with excitement. "It's Byron Gates."

"Oh." Vera felt a flush of embarrassment. Katherine had said the name as though she should have known the significance of one Byron Gates. But she had no idea.

"Byron Gates!" Katherine emphasized his last name.

Vera set her empty punch glass on a nearby windowsill beside two other abandoned glasses. "Gates. Gates. Hmmm."

Katherine nudged her. "From Gates Enterprises in Baltimore. You lived in Baltimore. Surely you know of the family." Her voice rose in pitch, colored with indulgence and impatience.

Chagrined, Vera thought until she remembered. "Come to

think of it, I do believe my employer in Baltimore was invited to their home for a reception once. But that reception was held in honor of people I didn't know, so I wasn't included. I never did learn more about the Gates family." She shrugged. "I was just a paid companion. I had no reason to socialize with them."

"Well, you do now." Katherine slipped a glance Byron's way. "I have a heart for no one but Christopher, but I would venture a guess that the other girls here would think you quite lucky."

"Lucky?"

"Yes. Haven't you seen how he's looked your way more than once tonight?"

Vera thought she had caught Byron stealing furtive glances at her as he maintained conversations with others. Until Katherine had mentioned it, Vera had attributed the observation to an overactive imagination. Or wishful thinking. "I've tried not to notice."

"He's noticed you. You know how love can catch one unawares. Deep feelings can start with just a look."

"Like with you and Christopher, perhaps?" Vera teased.

Katherine eyed her husband, standing at a small distance from them with a group of mutual friends. The love in her eyes surpassed all verbal expression. "Perhaps."

"Nevertheless, let us not speculate about love on my part or Byron's. I haven't so much as spoken to him yet. I might find him most disagreeable." She had a feeling she wouldn't.

"Once you stop swooning, you can decide." Katherine studied Byron from the corner of her eye. "I don't advise passing judgment based on someone's appearance because it's the heart that matters, but. . ."

"But?"

"He is dressed in quite a style and carries himself in a

manner that exudes confidence. Do you think he may be just a bit worldly?"

"Maybe a bit, at least in comparison to us out here in the country. Why do you mention it?" Vera asked.

"Just make sure he's not too worldly. I know you would never want to have a romantic relationship with someone who doesn't share your love for the Lord."

"True. I believe I would be much happier with a godly man," Vera answered with vigor.

"Good. That's what I knew you'd say." Katherine smiled. "Come now. Let's see Clarence."

"Clarence?" Vera studied the tall, dark-eyed man with chestnut brown hair. He stood erect, cocksure of himself as always. "What does he have to do with all this?"

"Everything. Byron is here visiting him."

"My, but you do work fast."

"Out of necessity," Katherine said. "Did you see Ethel watching him like she's an owl and he's a rat?"

Katherine wasn't certain she liked the idea of Byron being compared to a rat, but the allusion to prey wasn't lost on her. "Ethel eyes all the new men like that. And some of the old ones, too."

"I know." Katherine squeezed Vera's hand with urgency. "Let's show Mr. Byron Gates someone much prettier. There's no time to lose. Ethel is moving closer, as though she plans to strike any minute."

Vera looked toward her rival and saw that Katherine was right. Still, Vera tried not to look too eager. She did want to meet Byron but had no desire to run over top of Ethel to do it. Besides, Vera wasn't the most flamboyant woman in the room by any means. Certainly, someone with more fire in her appearance would attract a bachelor whose residence in Baltimore and association with Clarence suggested sophistication.

The closer they got to Byron, the faster Vera's heart beat. As Vera and Byron were introduced, she noticed Ethel casting a narrow-eyed look her way.

"I am enchanted to meet you," Byron said in greeting.

"Enchanté." She nodded and wondered how she had managed to form a welcome in French. If one was to utter a greeting comprised of only one word, at least the word should be sophisticated. She treated herself to silent congratulations.

He moved closer, bringing with him a clean scent of shaving tonic. "Ah, so you respond in French. Did you study abroad?" The way he cocked his chin in her direction showed that she had gotten his attention.

Vera suppressed a giggle. Study abroad! Hardly. She was merely a farm girl who was once a companion to an elderly Baltimore lady. Now she was home, helping her sister tend to her small son.

"Don't let her fool you with the errant foreign word. Vera's from around these parts, and she hasn't ventured far," Clarence offered. "The farthest she's ever been is from Hagerstown to Baltimore."

"Clarence," Katherine chastised him, "Vera may not have traveled far from this county, but she is able to hold her own against any sophisticate."

Clarence tilted his head and seemed to be holding back an urge to say something unpleasant. Vera tried not to wince. Obviously, Clarence wasn't thrilled by the prospect of her conversing with his friend from out of town.

"So you've been to Baltimore, eh?" Byron's eyes lit, and he focused his full attention on Vera. "Visiting friends?"

"I did more than visit." Despite Katherine's enthusiastic support and encouragement, Vera struggled to maintain a favorable posture and a lilt of confidence in her voice. "I lived with the Aldens."

"The Aldens." Byron gave the briefest of pauses before recalling the name. "You must mean the lawyer, Raleigh Alden, and his mother, June?"

Vera nodded and looked at the points of her shoes.

"Vera was June Alden's companion, but now she's home helping her sister, Alice," Katherine pointed out.

Vera was not ashamed of helping her sister. Still, she wished that her former status as nothing more than a paid companion had to be mentioned, June Alden's high regard for her notwithstanding. Vera held back another wince. Immediate honesty was the best policy.

There's no point in putting on airs, only to have the wind knocked out of my sails.

"Had I known the Aldens employed such a lovely companion, I might have ventured there a time or two myself," Byron told her.

Vera looked quickly into his blue eyes, then sent her gaze back down again. Byron was a bold one.

❧

Byron whistled as he made ready to retire for the night. He couldn't remember a time when he had met any woman in a church social setting who had captured his imagination with the liveliness of the delightful Vera Howard. In fact, he couldn't remember having been in a church setting lately. The thought shamed him.

No wonder he had recently felt his life spiraling downward. He remembered how he had been rebuffed by one of Baltimore's outstanding debutantes, a certain Miss Elizabeth Josephine Reynolds. Elizabeth wasn't the greatest prize of Baltimore society, so her rebuff of his advances had taken him aback. Her refusal hadn't been delivered with the practiced skill of a popular debutante, either. No, she had laughed in his face. Had he been such a rake as all that?

Apparently his reputation was not the best, and the social set in Baltimore knew it. He desired a woman of fine breeding and a high level of patience who would share his future responsibilities in running his father's manufacturing interests. Was this type of woman to be found?

He thought about his office and the responsibilities he had left at home. He wasn't afraid of work, but he wished the promised position offered more than worries and columns of numbers. The idea of sitting all day at a desk, working over accounts, managing inventory, vexing about how to keep workers happy with their pay while earning the company a profit, being sure the quality of goods was maintained, and then overseeing their shipment out from the Baltimore docks on time—none of these chores lent themselves to his particular interests or talents. Why couldn't his father have been a prosperous merchant so Byron could use his charm to sell fine goods? Or perhaps a lawyer with a position for Byron in his firm, since Byron could debate with the best of them?

Byron's father had already reminded him that his days of few responsibilities were numbered. "I am looking forward to passing the torch of Gates Enterprises to you, my eldest son. My boy who has grown into a fine specimen of a man."

As Father made the announcement, meant to be a supreme compliment, Byron had tried to appear enthusiastic. He even managed a smile. But his zest for running the family business ran cold.

Too restless to sleep, he took a seat in a corner chair and laid his head back against the leather. His thoughts wandered back to his childhood friend Daisy Estes. A man who flirted with as many women as Byron expected the occasional refusal, but he never worried. Not only did most women succumb to his engaging manner, but he also imagined that one day he could count on Daisy to marry him if all else failed. At least, that's what he had assumed for years, until he and Daisy realized one day that they could never step over the romantic line. Still, he felt hurt that she had turned her attentions to Horace Moore. Plain, dull Horace. Byron couldn't imagine his lively friend, so coquettish in her manner, saddled with such a bore. If she wouldn't become Mrs. Byron Gates, couldn't she at least have displayed better taste when she rebounded?

Even worse, he hated the thought of disappointing all four of their parents. The Estes and Gates families had always been friends, with the elders remarking what a fine match Byron and Daisy would make one day. They spoke not in jest.

Against his will, Byron recalled God's commandment: "Honour thy father and thy mother: that thy days may be long upon the land which the Lord thy God giveth thee."

Though his parents had no intention of forcing a marriage, Byron felt a sense of duty toward them. How could he, their eldest son and heir to the family business, not abide by their fondest wishes? As for being close to God—Byron had hardly been a monk, but he still kept the Lord's wishes in the back of his mind. Church teachings he learned as a boy were more than happy to oblige, popping into his head whether beckoned or not.

Clarence chose that moment to burst into the bedroom. "There you are, old man. I must say I'm surprised to find you here. I can't believe you are retiring for the night already. Unless you in fact plan to change clothes for another round of festivities."

"Festivities? Are you saying you know a place where celebrations of life are beginning anew?"

"I know of none. I was hoping you did."

"I'm not the one with connections here."

"True. No, old man, I'm afraid I know of no other place to go now. They roll the sidewalks up at five o'clock, to be sure. We must make our own entertainment out here in the country. Not that we're too shabby about that. But you can hardly expect our humble establishments to be as active as the big gaming halls and places of frolic that you might find in the city. In fact, by local standards a church social is considered a fine night of vigorous entertainment." Clarence sighed. "My, but I do miss the gala atmosphere of Baltimore."

"Yes, we did have a fine summer last year, didn't we? But surely you don't neglect to see the charms of your home."

Clarence surveyed the room and shrugged. "I suppose."

"I find the country quite charming indeed."

"Really? I'm surprised you're not bored already. Unless. . ." He sent Byron a cunning look. "You sly dog. You've found a woman, haven't you?"

two

Byron crossed his arms, shifted in his seat, and studied Clarence. As usual, his friend had ventured a correct guess. Relishing triumph, Byron allowed a smile to slip upon his countenance. "As a matter of fact, I have found a woman."

"I knew it!" Clarence rubbed his hands together and grinned. "I can see by the cat-that-swallowed-the-canary look on your face that you're confident she returns the favor. But why should I doubt it? You seem to find a woman anywhere you go." Since the bedroom had but one chair, he sat on the side of Byron's bed and positioned his foot on top of the mahogany rail left exposed by the blue bedspread.

"You exaggerate, my friend. I confess that this woman is not the usual type I pursue. She is very charming and a lovely woman indeed, yet in a way that displays no affectations." Byron looked into space, thinking of Vera. "I have drawn the distinct conclusion that this is one woman I shall never forget."

"A woman you shall never forget, eh?" Clarence rubbed his chin. "I'm thinking back on all the women you spoke with at the social."

"You'll be thinking a long time, then. People out here are quite friendly, and I spoke to many this evening."

Clarence chortled. "Friendly, yes. But I've never seen the women quite as friendly as they were tonight. They were drawn to you like bees to honey, old man. I can only stand nearby and hope some of your charm rubs off on me—or that I can be around to mend the hearts you break."

"You sell yourself short, Clarence. Besides, women—and fellows, as well—will always be fascinated by the new man in town. That's not to say you're old hat, but you certainly are well-known around these parts. I, on the other hand, am a stranger. To them, my story is new."

"Everything you say is indisputable. But remember, I've seen you operate in the city where you are well-known." He tilted his head and sent Byron a mischievous look. "I've always admired you for how you can charm any woman you have a mind to. So who is your latest victim?"

Byron felt the smile slide back to his feet. He cringed. "Victim?"

"A willing victim, no doubt," his friend hastened to assure him. "So who might the lucky woman be?"

Byron wished Clarence wasn't staring at him, waiting for an answer. So women associated with him were considered victims, eh? Byron resolved at that moment to improve his reputation. He took in a breath and held it as if to affirm his resolution.

"My, but she must be quite a prize. Let me guess." Clarence rolled his gaze upward and tapped his chin with his forefinger. "Is it Carolyn?" Clarence leveled his eyes toward Byron.

"The brunette with the red fan?"

"That's the one. She's quite a catch. I've had my eye on her myself for a while. I do say your appearance around these parts might liven things up and prod her not to wait too much longer to choose a suitor."

"She's that popular?"

"You didn't notice? She held court most of the night." Clarence smiled, and a mischievous twinkle sparked in his eyes. "I know. Maybe we can make a game of our little competition."

"Sorry, my friend, but we'll make no sport of Carolyn's

affections. No, I have someone else in mind."

"You want to make sport of another's affections?" Clarence shrugged. "One woman is as good as another for games, I suppose. Who, then?"

"No, I will not make sport of this woman's affections. I have resolved to change my ways."

Clarence whistled. "She must have made quite an impression."

"Yes. And I won't make sport of any woman's affections, for that matter."

"This change is quite sudden. I'm not sure I like it," Clarence said. "I'll take a guess. Is she a redhead?"

"No. She's a blond."

"A blond, eh? Now who could that be?" Clarence crossed his arms and thinned his lips in thought. A mischievous light struck his eyes as he snapped his fingers. "I know. It must be Rosetta."

"That harebrain?" Byron grimaced.

Clarence chuckled. "So she's witty. Then surely you must have your eye on Jane."

Byron shook his head.

Clarence let out an exasperated breath. "Then who, man? There was no other blond. At least, none worthy of the attentions of a man such as yourself."

"Really? If you think that, then surely you didn't see Vera Howard."

Clarence's mouth slackened. "Vera Howard? You must be out of your mind!"

"Why ever do you say that?"

"Because, she's. . .she's a wallflower, that's why. Hardly ever utters a word. As quiet as a church mouse. And speaking of church mice, Vera is certainly at home in a church. She's banging on the door every time it opens."

"Some men would consider quiet restraint an asset in a

woman and be delighted with a woman who considers church attendance more than a duty and an obligation—but a joy."

"I wouldn't take you for a man who values silence."

Byron bristled. "I'm not. And as long as I'm with Vera, I don't have to be. She and I had quite a lovely conversation."

"Indeed? Then her personality must undergo a transformation when she's with you. Not that I find such a development to be a complete surprise." He smirked. "Vera is inexperienced and no doubt flattered easily by your attentions. However, I must point out that she clearly is not your type."

Byron tried not to take offense at Clarence's observation. Though he knew his friend didn't mean to insult him, the truth hurt. He considered the possibility that the Lord was speaking to him. How long had He been trying to get Byron's attention? Too long, no doubt. Byron had finally reached the point where he was willing to listen, even if that meant he wouldn't like much of what he heard. "You were wrong about her being quiet, at least in my company."

Clarence shook his head. "Perhaps she seems talkative to you, but based on everything I've seen, she's a shy little thing. Don't take my word for it. You'll find out soon enough. The moment she slaps you across the cheek when you try to steal a kiss." He chuckled.

"Am I really such a rake as all that?"

"A rake? Why, many men don't mind wearing such a label. Don't you know the term holds a hint of intrigue and romance? Women love that sort of thing, you know."

"Women who care not a whit about home and family," Byron observed.

"Oh, so that's what you care about now, old man? Then maybe this mouse, Miss Vera Howard, would make you a fine, timid little wife."

"You need spectacles, my friend."

Clarence chuckled. "No indeed, my friend. You are the one who could use assistance with your vision and discernment. The apple of your eye tonight is dull. She is at present serving as a nanny to her infant nephew, Paul Victor, since her married sister, Alice, is once again in a family way."

"Alice Sharpe?"

Clarence nodded. "She'll be going into her confinement soon enough. And your Vera will be busier than ever."

"I'm sure she'll find plenty of time for me."

"Then you'd better hurry. Once Alice ties her down with two little brats, Vera will be hard-pressed to call her life her own. Not that she has much of a life now."

Byron opened his mouth to protest, but Clarence beat him to the punch. "I have a proposition for you."

"Oh?" Byron leaned forward in his chair.

Clarence hopped off the bed and moved closer to Byron. "I'll bet you can't get Vera to agree to marriage within six months."

"Marriage in six months? That's not a small wager."

"Not too large for a betting man such as yourself." Clarence leaned against the mahogany bedpost.

"I wish you wouldn't offer such temptation. You know my betting days are behind me. Even if they weren't, I could never toy with such a sweet woman as Vera."

"Toy with her? *Toy* is your middle name."

Byron swallowed. "But you know why I came here."

"To visit me, your old friend, of course." Clarence's tone told Byron he spoke only partly in jest.

"Of course. But also to cultivate new and better habits. I really do want to change."

"Perhaps, but that doesn't mean you must pursue the dullest woman in the county. You won't be happy if you're bored, and you'll only return to your old ways."

"But I won't be bored. My interest in Vera Howard is genuine. She intrigues me. And I plan to see if I can eventually coax her into a courtship."

Clarence laughed. "Surely you can't be serious."

"I am indeed."

"Suit yourself. But at least we can make the process more interesting."

Byron was almost afraid to ask. "How?"

"I'll make you a wager, but not a serious one. If you manage to begin courting Vera Howard within six months, I'll take you to a tavern at my expense to celebrate your victory."

The idea of betting on his future on a whim disgusted Byron, but he couldn't help himself. He had to learn the rest of Clarence's scheme. "And if I don't?"

His friend didn't hesitate. "You'll have to treat me to a night of gaming in Baltimore."

Byron didn't answer right away. Whether he won or lost the bet, he didn't want to go to either a tavern or on a night of gaming. He shook his head. "No. You can bet, my friend, but you'll be betting alone."

❧

"Bold, yes. Too bold if you ask me," Alice said a few days later after Vera told her about the encounter at the church social.

Each day, the two women took advantage of the quiet interlude after lunch dishes were gathered and washed. Usually, Vera enjoyed those moments of conversation and catching up with one another. But on this day, for the first time since her return to Washington County, Vera wished she had found something else to do instead of talking with Alice after lunch.

"Do you think such a sharp tone is good for the baby when you're trying to rock him to sleep?" Vera offered out of genuine concern and the desire to soften her sister's criticism.

"You're right." Alice looked up at Vera and then back to Paul. Rocking in the chair and holding him in a blue blanket, Alice looked as though she posed for a talcum powder advertisement.

Vera rocked back and forth in the chair across from Alice. "I don't know. I rather liked Mr. Gates's straightforwardness. After all, it's not every day I meet a new man who is free with compliments."

"Free with flattery for you and every other woman who crosses his path, I'll venture," Alice cautioned.

"I'm not sure I would pass such judgment yet. I may not be the most beautiful woman in any given gathering, but surely you don't mean that I am so ugly that no man would flatter me." Vera picked up a ball of twine and a tiny crochet hook from the basket beside the chair.

"Of course not, sister dear. I didn't mean to hurt you. I just am very aware that you aren't wise in the ways of the world and of men." Alice rubbed her son's cheek.

"And you are?" As soon as she blurted out the words, regret filled her soul. "I'm sorry. I didn't mean that."

"I know." Alice looked up and sighed. "I suppose I would have been more insulted had you implied that I know all too much about men. Besides, we are sisters, and if we cannot be frank with one another, then we don't have much of a relationship, do we?"

Vera tried to concentrate on a stitch, but in her distress, her work wasn't up to its usual quality. "It would break my heart for that to be so."

"Then let me continue to be forthcoming with the truth for your own good. How much do you know about Byron Gates?"

"Not much," she admitted. "Only that he's charming and handsome. Quite pleasant, really."

"Of course he is. He's a carefree bachelor. No doubt he uses smooth words to captivate all the ladies. And that is why, my dear sister, he is not a suitable match for you," Alice cautioned. "I advise you to stay away from Byron, and I expect you to heed that advice."

"How do you know so much about him?"

"After you mentioned him to me on the evening of the social, I had Elmer do some digging for me."

"Alice! You certainly didn't waste any time. Why are you worried? I don't even know Byron. At least not very well." Vera tore out the stitch she had just crocheted.

"True, but you have never expressed interest in any man before now."

"That's just what Katherine said," Vera noted.

"And she is a lifelong friend of yours. So you can see why I believe that my fears are not unfounded."

"Fears?"

"Yes." Alice sighed, a sad look reaching into her eyes. "I'm afraid I don't like what Elmer told me about your Mr. Gates."

"What did he discover?"

"Byron Gates is a known rake, cad, and gambler. No honest woman in Baltimore will have him, and neither should you. I recommend strongly that you stay away from him. And Elmer agrees."

Vera didn't answer. She could only hope the reports about Byron were wrong.

three

Later that night, Vera thought about her sister's admonition. Though the Sharpes lived in the country, Elmer had friends nearby who once lived in the city, and they would be in the know about Baltimore's prominent families. Vera had no reason to doubt that what he had discovered about Byron held the truth. Surely his reputation as a rake and gambler was deserved.

Vera let out a distressed sigh. She had seen handsome faces and even *bon vivants* before, but Byron possessed an indefinable quality that attracted her. And yes, she was naive about men. No wonder her sister had expressed concern about her becoming involved with Byron Gates. But Vera didn't lack discernment and wisdom.

I don't care what Alice says. If Byron comes to church this Sunday, that will show me and everyone else that he is nurturing his spiritual life. I don't care what his reputation is. I want to find out about him for myself. I'm going to talk to him anyway.

❧

Vera looked out over the lush, Maryland countryside that was the Sharpes' farm. Her sister had finally permitted her to accept Byron's request to share a picnic lunch, however grudgingly, as long as she and the baby accompanied them. Over the past few weeks, Vera had noticed that Byron never seemed to miss a chance to converse with her at church and to hover nearby at local social gatherings. Though to be bold was not her way, Vera gave him enough encouraging glances that he finally asked her if she'd consent to promenade with him on the next sunny day. To her surprise, Alice and Elmer gave their permission that night. She remembered writing a reply to Byron's request, which contained her pledge to prepare a basket lunch.

Vera peeked at her sister. Despite her reluctance to allow Byron near Vera, Alice had been kind enough to keep herself out of earshot most of the day. Yet she lingered closely enough to the couple on their outing that there would be no question they were fully chaperoned and that all was proper. Her infant son, Paul, had proven to be an agreeable and quiet companion. Sitting underneath an oak tree, Alice played with him, cooing all the while. Seeing the picture of her sister's happiness, Vera couldn't help but fantasize about what her own eventual marriage and motherhood would be like.

"I do believe this is the best fried chicken I ever put in my mouth, Miss Howard."

She regarded her own leg of fried chicken. The coating had cooked to a golden brown, and pinprick-sized dots of black pepper promised a well-seasoned entrée. The juicy meat didn't disappoint. Though she knew a compliment was deserved, she wasn't sure how to respond to such hyperbole. "Indeed, sir? Then you must not have eaten too much chicken in your lifetime."

"I beg your pardon, but I have," he responded without a shade of defensiveness. "I am quite well traveled. Would you like me to tell you all about Spain?"

Spain! Imagine, being so well traveled. She thought about her own sheltered life and how she had seen nothing outside of her beloved Maryland. How could she expect to keep a worldly man such as Byron interested in her trivial doings? Then she remembered sage advice given by Aunt Middie long ago: *To be fascinating, open your ears and use them!*

Vera leaned closer but made a conscious effort not to lean

too near. "Yes, I would love to hear about Spain."

He launched into a fascinating account of the sights of the distant land and moved on to descriptions of other places about which Vera had learned only in books. By account's end, she was shaking her head in amazement. "How marvelous to be so well traveled."

Byron looked into the sky. "But I have so many other places I want to go. Greece, Cyprus, Egypt."

Vera caught her breath. "I can only dream of such strange lands."

"Then dream with me." He looked at her, but his tone took on a faraway pitch, as though he were traveling to a place beyond their immediate circumstances and taking her with him.

The thought gave her goose bumps. "Oh, how I would love to dream with you."

Propping himself on one palm, he tilted himself closely enough to her that she could breathe in the scent of his manly shaving water. That he desired to bring himself closer to her filled her with vitality. She could feel her eyes open wide with interest.

"I can show you the world if you're willing to go along with me," he persuaded.

Vera took a sudden interest in her buttered yeast roll. She could never travel with her lunch companion except as Mrs. Byron Gates, and it was much too soon for either of them to contemplate such a proposal.

His voice retained persuasiveness. "You would like to travel, wouldn't you, Miss Howard?"

She bit into her roll with what she hoped looked like a ladylike motion. She could only imagine listening to his soft, masculine voice telling her the history of each landmark.

"Certainly you would," he answered for her.

"One day, perhaps," she managed.

"I can't say that I blame you for not wanting to commit to me as a traveling companion—yet. Perhaps we might take some time to learn more about each other." He drew his hand closer to hers but stopped short of touching it.

Vera shot a glance toward Alice. Almost as though she knew Vera's thoughts, Alice gave her a warning look. Vera couldn't decide whether to move her hand back to the folds of her skirt. She looked into Byron's face and decided to keep her fingers right where they were. She cleared her throat. "How?"

"I suppose you have observed that I haven't let you out of my sight whenever we're in the same room together."

Vera giggled, drawing Alice's unwanted attention once more. Vera averted her eyes and set their gaze upon her linen-clad knees. "I would not be so immodest as to think you were so very interested in me."

My, but he must think me a ninny from the way I sound! She held back a cringe.

He chuckled, filling the air with the mirth of kindness. "Immodest? Why, I should think you have suitors standing in line."

A shiver of pleasure coursed through her upon hearing such flattery. Vera lifted her lace fan and waved it before her face, even going so far as to bat her eyelashes. She had never flirted so boldly before, but try as she might, she couldn't stop herself. "I can see why you are such a popular bachelor in Baltimore. Surely the ladies there swoon over you."

To her surprise, he tensed. His countenance took on a hard expression, and he turned his gaze from her face, looking instead at a distant grove of trees. She followed his stare but saw nothing out of the ordinary that would call his attention to the foliage. Fear shot through her as she placed the fan back on the blanket.

"Is anything the matter, Byron?"

He looked at her, but his eyes appeared to be vacant, as though he didn't really see her. "No." His tone wasn't convincing.

"I—I'm so sorry. You must think me much too bold and brash. It. . .it's much too brisk today for a fan. I don't even know why I brought it."

"Perhaps you care to fan away the rumors about me that you obviously heard?"

"Rumors?" she blurted.

"Now you're the one who's being coy."

She set down her fan and looked at him without smiling. "All right. It's true. I have heard that you are quick to flirt with many women and that your favorite pastime is gaming."

"And yet you still don't mind sharing lunch with me?" He searched her face with a probing look.

She averted her gaze to the blanket and then looked back at him. "Was I a fool to take a risk?"

"I hope not. In fact, I am hoping to prove to you and the rest of the world—and even more importantly, to God—that I want to come back to the fold."

Her heart beat with happiness. "Really?"

"Yes. I regret my youthful follies. Not to mention, I have grown tired of them. As the apostle Paul wrote in his letters, there comes a time when a man must put away childish things. And while gaming and flirting might seem to be adult pursuits, they are childish."

She took a moment to contemplate his words. "Perhaps with wisdom so hard won, you should consider the ministry."

His laugh sounded pleasant. "I am neither called to nor worthy of such a high pursuit. However, your compliment will be one I shall revisit in my memory many times." He grew serious. "Thank you for your willingness to show me a Christian spirit, flawed as my past is, when surely your past, present, and future are—and will be—as white as a fresh cotton sheet on a summer day."

"Now you are the one who places too high a regard on a person." Unaccustomed to such flattery, she waved her fan in front of her cheeks once more.

"Are we experiencing a sudden rash of heat?" he teased.

The flush of warmth she felt made the fan even more necessary. "Yes. Yes we are experiencing a sudden rash of heat."

"Really?"

"I assure you I never play the coquette. At least, I never normally do. I mean, I didn't until today. I—I. . .oh, I don't know what I mean." Waves of chagrin flowed through her. She couldn't look at him, not at all. She rose to her feet. "If you're done with your meal, I suppose we had better be packing up what remains of the lunch. The baby needs to go down for his afternoon nap soon."

❧

Returning to Clarence's from the picnic, Byron didn't hurry the horse. He wanted to contemplate the time he has just spent with Vera. Even though her sister had been within earshot, entertaining the baby, he could sense that Vera's emotions toward him grew. Based on what Clarence had revealed about her and given Vera's expressed chagrin at being just a mite coy that afternoon, she wasn't one to flirt indiscriminately. He had found her expressions beautiful and her witticisms fascinating. Having always protected his heart, Byron didn't remember a time he had known love—at least, not the kind of love that could sustain a marriage. But Vera was unique. Whenever he neared her, he could envision wanting to stay with her for a long, long time.

If only he had not been so quick to throw away a perfectly respectable reputation with shenanigans well-known to all. How could someone such as Vera be expected to think of him as anything but a cad—a man entirely unsuitable for her?

Try as he might, he had become all too aware that ridding himself of his past mistakes was not going to be easy. People with vicious tongues, jealous of the Gates family's position and wealth, were all too eager to keep accounts of indiscretions alive. Would his past one day catch up with him, sweeping Vera from him?

Even worse, Byron knew his family had other plans for him. Plans he didn't much care to have come to fruition. He didn't see how Vera, a countrywoman not raised to join his social set, could possibly fit in that picture.

Turning into Clarence's drive, Byron tried to put on a happy face. No point in sharing his worries with his friend. He had a feeling they would come home to roost soon enough.

❧

Alice said nothing during the journey from the picnic place to the farmhouse. If anything, she demonstrated the epitome of the charmed matron as long as Byron remained in their company. Only later, after Vera had bid Byron good afternoon and Alice had put down her child for a nap, did she seek out Vera in the informal parlor.

"There you are. You seem chipper." Alice took a seat in the overstuffed brown chair across from Vera's.

"I'm always chipper." Vera ran her feather duster over the lampshade with more enthusiasm than she usually displayed for dusting.

"Not quite as chipper as you are today. So tell me, what puts you in such a good mood? Or shall I say, who?" Alice inclined her head in Vera's direction. "Let me guess. Byron Gates is responsible for your carefree demeanor."

Vera sat in a convenient chair but kept the feather duster in her hand. "I confess it. Byron is the source of my pleasure."

"And many other women's. I knew that letting you picnic with him was a mistake. I pray you haven't fallen into his treacherous web."

"How can you discern that he has woven such a web? You hardly know him. I daresay you don't know him as well as I do."

"Not that your acquaintance is one of longevity."

"True." Vera flinched.

"I'm sorry, but I worry because of Byron's sudden eagerness to court you."

Vera fingered the crocheted doily on the right arm of the chair and studied the pattern. "You think he will ask to court me in earnest?"

"In earnest, you say. That only proves you have been contemplating the possibility."

Vera looked back to her sister's face. "What if I have? Am I such an ugly ninny that no man would ever want to court me? Is that what you think?"

"You know that's not what I think. Granted, you know as well as I do that you have a reputation as a wallflower, but many a wallflower has journeyed to matrimony with great success. So please, humor me, will you, dear? Let me have Elmer ask Clarence if Byron's intentions are honorable. Our families are both on friendly terms, and I know Clarence would have no reason to lie. Elmer, I assure you, will find out all we need to know with the greatest discretion."

"I don't know. . . ."

Alice leaned toward Vera and set her gaze into her eyes. "What are you afraid of? That your new interest is not as honorable as you hope?"

Vera held Alice's gaze but rooted her heel in the floor. "No. I am not afraid. Have Elmer ask him. And I want to know as soon as possible what Clarence has to say."

four

The following day, Byron returned to the Stanley house from an errand in town. To his surprise, Clarence greeted him at the door with the air of a child awaiting a gift from a doting grandparent. "You'll never guess what happened today."

"I don't know, but I can say you look happy." Byron hurried up the porch steps and tried to think of what event could put such a smile on Clarence's face. "Perhaps someone who owed you a debt came by to repay?"

"Now that would have been good news. But sadly, that isn't so."

"What, then?"

"Perhaps you'd better sit down." Clarence gestured his friend inside. "Let's take a seat in my study."

Byron followed Clarence to a room where he had traveled many times—the study near the back of the house. Stale tobacco smoke and the scent of Clarence's usual citrus shaving lotion mingled to remind visitors that the room was his haunt. He took a seat in his favorite black leather chair, and Byron selected a Chippendale intended for visitors.

The suspense was weighing on Byron. "All right, tell me."

Clarence lit his pipe. "Byron, my good man, you are obviously making serious progress with our wager on Miss Vera Howard."

The news was welcome to Byron, but he tried not to convey any emotion. "What do you mean?"

"I mean, I had a visit from her brother-in-law today. Elmer Sharpe."

"Oh." Byron's voice sounded flat, even to his ears. This had happened before. First he would garner the attention of an attractive woman, enjoy a mild flirtation, and then a key relative would get wind of his attentions and ask probing questions. More often than not, such a visit signaled the end of his tête-à-tête with the woman in question. "What did he want?"

"I'll give you three guesses, and the first two don't count. He wanted to know if I think your intentions toward Vera are honorable."

Byron remembered Clarence's insistence on betting. He held his breath and tightened his fingers around the chair arms. "So what did you tell him?"

Clarence inhaled on his pipe and then refreshed the tobacco with a light. The aroma of quality leaves filled the study. "I'm your friend, am I not?"

"Yes. So what did you say?"

"Do you think I'm a fool, man? I told him that of course your intentions are honorable."

Byron brightened. "You did?"

Clarence laughed. "You sound like a little boy on Christmas Day."

Byron wondered if the comparison was all too apt. "I do thank you for speaking kindly of me to Vera's brother-in-law."

"Kindly. Yes." Clarence smirked. "Oh, I feel badly about my little fib, but it's all in good fun."

"But Clarence, you did not tell a fib. My intentions toward Vera are indeed honorable. She means more to me than just a little fun. I've told you that."

Clarence looked down his pipe stem at Byron. "I feel sorry for you, then. Her sister isn't going to be happy about the prospect of your courting Vera. Granted, I sang your praises, but Elmer is quite astute. No doubt his visit here was prompted by whatever he heard about your past. I also have no doubt that he'll share whatever he finds out about you with his wife."

"Oh." Byron stared at his boots.

"You have a right to be disconcerted," Clarence admitted. "Alice is very protective of Vera. You'll have a long row to hoe indeed to get on her good side."

ꜟ

Vera sat at the table and watched an argument ensuing in the kitchen of the Sharpe farm. Alice pressed her fingers into a mound of dough with vigor. She refused to turn her eyes toward her husband.

"I don't care what Clarence says, Byron Gates is known as a man about town in Baltimore, and I see no reason to think he's changed just because he's in the country. If anything, he's liable to believe our Vera is more naive than the women in the city, and he'll try to take advantage of her just as sure as the sun will rise tomorrow."

"Now, now, Alice." Elmer consoled her from his place at the table. "You don't know that. Perhaps Byron has come here as part of a process of invoking real change in his life."

"And you don't know that," she retorted.

Up to this point, Vera had witnessed the exchange as she deboned chicken for use in a rice dish. She set down the butcher knife. "Please don't be vexed, Alice. You need to take care of yourself and of the life you carry."

"It's too late. I'm already vexed." Alice kept kneading the dough.

Elmer intervened. "Vera is right. Alice, I know you are not yourself thanks to your delicate condition, but please, do not resort to histrionics in an effort to control your sister. She has served you well all this time. Isn't she allowed to find a little happiness for herself if that's God's will?"

Vera never expected to find such a strong ally in her brother-in-law. She let out a little gasp. "Thank you, Elmer."

"I would think my own husband would defend my viewpoint," Alice rebuked him, her eyes narrowed. "With his reputation, Byron Gates surely is not the man for our Vera."

"Alice, I know you want what's best for Vera, but you also want what's best for our children. You're worried about losing her, aren't you?" Elmer looked at Vera.

Alice nodded. "All right, I'll admit it. I don't want to lose Vera." Alice looked at Vera, her eyes soft with the love and concern of a sister. "Can you blame me?"

Vera responded to Alice with a loving look in return, though she remained silent.

"Of course I don't blame you for not wanting Vera to leave," Elmer agreed. "But we can hire a nanny if need be."

"How can you be so callous?" Alice asked. "A nanny would never love our children as much as their own flesh-and-blood aunt! Isn't that right, Vera?" Alice's large eyes reminded Vera of a sad puppy.

"Of course, that's right." Vera swallowed and kept her focus on the chicken. Leaving the love and security she enjoyed at her sister's house was a drawback to any romance she might find, but if she was ever to have her own life, she would have to look at the transition as a new and exciting step in God's promise for her future.

Elmer raised his hands in mock exasperation and let them fall back on his lap. "Women!"

The sisters chuckled, but as soon as the moment passed, Vera turned to serious contemplation. *Father in heaven, do not let me become a source of contention between this couple Thou hast joined together. I am torn about my feelings for Byron and my place in Thy world. Please show me what is Thy will.*

"What are you thinking, Vera?" Alice interrupted.

"I was praying."

"You'll be needing lots of prayer if you think you can tame Byron Gates." Alice stopped working the dough long enough to study Vera. "Surely I'm not the only person you've talked to about Byron. You're so enamored that you can hardly contain yourself."

"Have I been as silly as all that?" Vera set a leg bone on the table.

"Perhaps not," Alice admitted. "But have you talked about Byron to anyone else?"

She stopped her task long enough to consider the question. "I did mention Byron to Katherine."

"And what did she have to say?"

Vera didn't answer right away. "Well, she did say he's quite handsome."

"Even the men have noticed that," Elmer noted. "Whenever Gates enters a room, the other young bachelors look at him with daggers in their eyes. I'd say they view him as unwelcome competition, to be sure."

"I don't mind admitting that Mr. Gates is handsome, although he wouldn't hold any appeal for me even if I were still single," Alice said. "But whatever your opinion of his countenance and form, appearances are not everything."

"I agree," Vera said, "and I would never choose a companion based on attractiveness alone. Katherine knows that."

"So Katherine had no reservations?" Alice stopped manipulating the dough.

Vera swallowed. "I wish I didn't have to tell you this, but as soon as she saw Byron's worldly appearance and bearing, she advised me to be sure he loves the Lord before I become too attached to the idea of romance."

"I knew Katherine to be wise. Good for her for speaking the truth." Alice smiled and rolled the dough into a ball.

"Byron told me during the picnic that he wants his mistakes to stay in the past and that he wants to pursue a closer relationship with God. No doubt that since he'll be seeking God, his behavior will adjust itself accordingly and will be above reproach now and in the future. True, it is never wise to stray from God, but judging from Byron's attitude, he has repented and is eager to return to God's standards for his life. And as for me, I want to give him a chance."

Vera remembered the picnic, and how Byron's presence had made her tremble with delight. "I may as well tell you that I did invite him to accompany me to church as long as he remains here."

"Church, eh?" Elmer laughed and looked at his wife. "I don't see how you can object to that, Alice."

She shot her husband a look. "I do not approve. Ensuring oneself of a regular escort is fine and good for a young woman, but Byron's presence is sure to discourage more fitting suitors."

"It's just church," Elmer countered, "and no other suitors have made their intentions known."

Vera felt the sting of Elmer's comment.

"It's not as though Mr. Gates made himself known. You had to seek out Clarence to learn his opinion of Mr. Gates's intentions, remember?"

"Of course." Elmer's voice displayed uncharacteristic irritability. "Instead of complaining, Alice, you should be thanking me that I sought to protect Vera from any man who might be using worship in the Lord's house as a ruse for meaningless flirtation."

"I don't think he is. As I said, he really is trying to change," Vera volunteered.

"That's what Clarence indicated, as well," Elmer agreed. "Gates's willingness to turn away from a sinful life should make you happy, Alice."

"Of course I'm happy for him," Alice agreed. "But, Vera, I doubt that the Lord expects you to take every errant sinner you meet under your wing."

"I'm not taking every errant sinner under my wing," Vera replied. "Just Byron."

❧

Late Wednesday afternoon, Byron entered the dining room of the Stanley house for dinner. He was surprised to find Clarence reading a newspaper at the table. Normally, he had left for his card game by this hour. "Good afternoon, Clarence."

Upon spying his friend, Clarence set the paper on the table and studied him. "What brings you to the table so early?"

"I might ask you the same question."

Clarence shrugged. "Coughs and colds kept two of our card players away. We called off the games." He peered at Byron. "Your turn."

Byron slid onto his seat and nodded to the servant to fetch his drink. "Midweek church service. I don't want to be late."

"Church? On Wednesday night?" Clarence asked Byron. "Since when do you care about going to church in the middle of the week? Isn't once a week enough to fulfill one's religious obligation?"

"I wouldn't call my attendance an obligation at all. I find it rather pleasurable." Byron straightened his tie. "Especially since I discovered that Vera attends midweek services."

Clarence leaned his chin against his palm. "So from now on you'll be going twice a week."

"I've been going twice a week. You just haven't noticed."

"I noticed you've been turning down my invitations to

Wednesday evening card games. Now I know why. But church, old man?" Clarence tugged at his collar as though the motion would help more air enter his lungs. "Stifling."

"Am I right in assuming you don't care to join me?"

"Right you are." He leaned back in his seat as a servant set down a bowl of squash soup before him.

"Too bad. You might meet a woman there yourself."

"I know all the women in that church, and I have since I was a boy. There's no fresh face there for me."

"Then go for the sermons," Byron suggested as he was served his own bowl of soup. "Even in midweek, they are quite inspiring. I didn't know the Bible contained such depth. There's much more to it than the Ten Commandments."

"As if you could recite even five of them."

"I can now."

Clarence shook his head. "I'm astounded. And this is all because of Vera Howard. Whatever do you see in that little mouse?"

"If you have to ask, you don't understand love."

"Love?" Clarence chortled. "Isn't it a little too soon to call whatever it is you're feeling love?"

Byron realized that, according to convention, he shouldn't be blurting his realization of such potent feelings even to his best friend. The thought occurred to him that giving his feelings such weight was premature. But he knew that whenever he came near to Vera, he lost all sense of place and time. Only she, with her beauty and sweet spirit, existed for him. As long as he could see her, little else mattered to him. No other woman had made him feel that way. Not even Daisy, whom he had known since childhood.

"Most likely you would label my feelings infatuation," Byron conceded to Clarence. "And perhaps they started out that way.

I did feel an initial flush of longing when we first met. Yet this time, it's different. Unlike my notice of ladies in Baltimore, with Vera I am not ready to give her up and move on my next—and more compliant—conquest. I would like to remain with Vera as long as I can."

"Forever?"

"I cannot say so yet. But I do find her intriguing. She's unlike any other woman I've met."

"You keep saying that, but you can't prove it by me."

"Must I prove anything to you, Clarence? Really, she is pure and sweet and beautiful in a wholesome way."

"Wholesome. Not a quality you usually look for in a woman, and certainly not one I seek."

"Then maybe if you gave someone like Vera a chance, you'd appreciate a woman who listens to your stories. Vera always listens to mine." Byron smiled, remembering how mesmerized she had been by his accounts of foreign travel.

"I wonder how long that will last?"

"You are too cynical."

"I prefer to think of my attitude as one of caution. What if you flirt with her and you discover she's not the lady you thought her to be?"

"She is every bit an innocent," Byron protested with more might than he intended. "You, having known her all her life, should be aware of that."

Clarence shrank. "Yes. All right, I admit it. If you were to discover anything sullied about Vera Howard, I would be shocked."

"So how can you even suggest she's anything but the greatest of ladies? Why, if you weren't my friend, I would acquaint you with my fist for giving expression to such a thought."

"I understand that you're not yourself, befuddled as you are by Vera, but I've seen women like her before, and so have you. A member of the fairer sex who has little experience can often become enraptured by the attentions of a man of the world. She thinks she wants to remain virtuous but is soon swept away by his charms, and then. . ." He let his voice taper and then sighed as though he were remembering a few misadventures of his own. "If you can convince her you're in love, you may be in for a most interesting evening."

"With some of the women I've known in Baltimore, perhaps. But Vera won't be as willing to part with her virtue in exchange for a few sweet words."

Clarence thought for a moment. "I do admit, Vera is more devout than most. You're in for a challenge, my good man. Perhaps that's why you find her to be such an intriguing enigma."

five

Later that evening, Byron arrived at the Sharpe farm to drive Vera to church. She greeted him at the door, looking ravishing as always. By this time, he knew the color of all her dresses, and tonight she had donned his particular favorite, a pink frock that made her blond locks seem brighter, brought out the roses in her cheeks, and nipped her small waist.

Lest he make her feel uncomfortable, he didn't allow his appreciative gaze to linger on her too long. "I'm here yet again to drive a beautiful lady to church. Byron Gates, reliable escort extraordinaire!" He bent low at the waist and swept his arm in a grand gesture, hat in hand.

"A beautiful lady?" Vera blushed.

"Yes, you and no one else." His voice softened, and he drank in Vera's loveliness until he felt the presence of another. He looked beyond Vera to see her sister standing a few feet away in the parlor, holding the baby. Her expression was hardly agreeable. "Good evening, Mrs. Sharpe."

"Good evening." Spoken through tightened lips, the salutation sounded forced.

Her terse expression surprised him, since Vera's sister had been pleasant immediately after the picnic. And Clarence promised that he had praised Byron when Elmer made inquiries.

Still, Byron had been greeted in such a manner before in houses where he was wearing out his welcome. Had he already stepped over the line with the Sharpes? Or had his reputation merely preceded him? He decided not to consider either possibility, especially since he had been a gentleman at the picnic and committed no romantic crime by escorting Vera to and from church each week.

Elmer emerged from another part of the house. "Good evening, Byron." Elmer's tone conveyed warmth, the type of warmth that told him that he understood Byron. Had he been as much of a rogue in his younger days as Byron had been? Byron couldn't be sure, but he was glad to have an ally. An important one at that.

"Good evening to you, Elmer. I trust all went well with the birth of the new foal last night."

"Yes, though for a while it was touch and go. But the little horse is a beauty, just like his mother."

"Indeed." Byron remembered another beauty. He gazed once more at Vera, the lovely blond before him. He couldn't help but find her tempting. Yes, he had come to rural Maryland to change, to rid himself of his roguish ways. So why had he run into Vera? Was she really so appealing, or was he simply too attracted to women of any persuasion to know what—or who—was right?

He could meditate on the possibilities all day and never find the answer, so he decided to focus on the present. "We had best be leaving, lest we be late for the service."

"Yes, I do hate to walk in late," Vera agreed.

As they traversed the lawn, he halfway listened to her talk as he helped her onto the buggy for their brief journey to church. The habit of lending only a fraction of his attention was a practiced skill he had developed from listening to many women chatter. He found most of them to be content with the occasional nod, making him wonder whether they cared if he listened to them or not. Just as he granted himself a mental pat on the back for his sly ways, guilt stabbed him. Hadn't he just thought to himself how he found Vera fascinating? Then he should be willing to listen to her. At that moment, he vowed to mend his ways.

Open ears offered a pleasant surprise. Vera proved herself well versed on the topics of the day, and even offered opinions that could stand up to logic. Not like the other women he'd known. His off-and-on attention in the past had yielded information about Paris fashions and the cost of Irish lace. Vera didn't seem to concern herself with such trivialities, yet her style of dress looked impeccable. Even better, Vera sought and listened to his thoughts and opinions. She grew more fascinating by the moment.

They reached a point of companionable silence, a fact that didn't bother him and didn't seem to vex her, either. With a side-glance, he observed the sheen of her blond tresses, the high color in her cheeks, and the enthusiastic turn of her pouty lips. Temptation reached fiery tentacles around him.

He wondered if she struggled, too. He suspected she did. More than once, he had caught her viewing him, then looking away so quickly that he knew she hoped he hadn't noticed. Blushes and intense fanning were other indicators to him that Vera burned hot underneath her cool exterior. Reading such hints had become an accomplishment, one that served him well as he pursued flirtations in the past. Remembering they were on their way to church, he resisted the urge to pull the carriage off on a grassy patch on the side of the path so he could kiss her.

"A penny for your thoughts," she ventured.

He startled. "A mere penny?"

She laughed softly. "I might have more in my purse, but I would hate to divert money from the collection plate."

"Well, we can't have that, now can we? Especially for such

a poor investment as the content of my thoughts." He turned serious. "I doubt you'd want to know what I'm thinking."

"Oh, but I do." Her eyes widened.

"What would you say if I told you I was thinking about what it might be like to kiss you?"

She gasped, her expression a mixture of pleasure, surprise, and uncertainty. "Mr. Gates! Are you always so bold?"

He sent her his most appealing sideways grin. "I find I am not bold at all in the presence of homely women."

She fanned herself and stared at passing trees. "I do not give out my favors frivolously. Not even for a comely and sophisticated man such as yourself."

"I know you don't. That fact makes you all the more appealing in my eyes."

She fanned herself with renewed vigor. "I declare, how you do make me blush!"

"So there is a bit of the coquette in you, after all."

"The coquette in me doesn't show herself too often. In fact, she can disappear just like that." Vera closed her fan with a decisive snap and placed it in her lap. "Now to be perfectly serious. I will not kiss anyone but the man who will one day be my husband."

"Really?" Relief that Clarence was wrong about Vera's fortitude as well as a feeling of disappointment presented themselves. He covered his inner turbulence with a quip. "What a quaint notion."

"I don't find it quaint at all. Good morals are always in style," she pointed out.

He noted the white clapboard building on the horizon, its painted steeple pointing toward heaven. "Indeed. I suppose our timely arrival at church is proof positive of that fact."

"Yes, and not a moment too soon, either."

"Now really, I am not uncouth," he assured her. "And to prove my point, I promise to be the perfect gentleman from now on. I won't even broach the subject of a kiss again without your leave."

"If I were playing the coquette, I would venture the observation that your resolution is regrettable."

"Yes, it is." He tried to keep his stare from her full lips. "Regrettable indeed."

❧

Clarence was waiting for Byron when he returned from escorting Vera to church. He sat on the porch, rocking back and forth, and motioned for Byron to join him. "So how did things go with the little mouse?"

He flinched and then leaned into a porch column rather than taking comfort in sitting in an available wicker chair. "I wish you wouldn't call her that."

"Call her what?"

"A mouse, of course. Must you sound so condescending?"

"So sorry, old man." A twitch of his lips revealed Clarence's apology was less than sincere. "So how did it go? Did you kiss her?"

Byron debated whether or not to tell Clarence the awful truth. Not so long ago, he wouldn't have hesitated to change the subject, or even to exaggerate so it would appear that Vera couldn't resist his substantial charms. "I didn't try."

"You didn't try?" Clarence didn't bother to conceal his shock.

Byron folded his arms. "No. I broached the subject, but she wasn't willing. I promised I'd be the perfect gentleman, and I will continue to do so."

Clarence sniffed. "I would think someone as naive as Miss Howard would have fainted with delight at the prospect of your attentions. Surely you are not losing your touch?"

Byron bristled in spite of himself. "Vera is not just any woman. She's different from the others, just as I told you. Her refusal only proves me right."

Clarence chuckled. "You had better hope she's not too different. Or else you'll lose the bet."

"I've told you, there is no bet." Byron's voice sounded as irritated as he felt. He stopped himself before he could say anything he might regret.

Clarence laughed and rose from his seat. "Come on in, old man. Let's call it a night."

Byron made a show of looking at the stars. "In just a moment."

"Planning your next strategy?"

"No, I'm only gathering my thoughts."

Clarence shrugged. "Whatever you say. Are you and I still meeting tomorrow morning for our horseback ride?"

"Of course. I'm looking forward to that."

Byron turned to look at the night sky and heard the door shut behind his friend. The solitude left him with a sense of freedom and weightiness combined. He prayed he hadn't offended Vera with his boldness. For the first time, he noticed that he truly was concerned about his behavior in relation to a woman—Vera.

Lord, guide my relationship with Vera.

He took in a breath. Had he just prayed? How many years had transpired since he tried to communicate with God? Hadn't he been a boy wearing pajamas, kneeling by the bed? He remembered the simple prayer his mother listened to each night. "Bless Mama. Bless Papa. Bless Katie. Bless Jenny. Bless Billy. Bless Gertie. Bless Bobby. And bless Bitsie. And thank Thee for Thy gracious mercy. I ask Thee in the name of Thy Son, Jesus. Amen."

Byron grinned. His parents were both blessed with good health despite their advanced years, still abiding in that same house. His brothers and sisters—now known as Katherine, Virginia, William, Gertrude, and Robert—were grown and living in various forms of contentment. Long ago, the cat had met her reward—a paradise of soft pillows and unlimited catnip and cream, according to Mother.

Ah, for those years of untarnished joy. Perhaps that's what Vera possessed that appealed to him so much, aside from her obvious physical attributes. The beauty of fresh innocence. He realized more than ever that he would not be the one to sully such loveliness in any way.

six

Days later, Vera quivered with anticipation as she and Byron approached the Sharpes' house after the Sunday morning worship service. Looking at her lap, she was pleased to see that her blue summer frock looked fresh despite the heat. Only two small strands had freed themselves from her chignon. She consoled herself with the hope that they didn't make her appear too mussed.

She stole a glance at Byron. He appeared as handsome as ever, with his refined good looks and posture that bespoke genuine confidence. On their last encounter, she had summoned all of her strength of will not to allow him to kiss her, and she knew she had to be vigilant in resisting his charms. Would he try to kiss her again? She hoped so. And she hoped not. For if he did, she didn't know what she might do.

Lord, grant me strength.

The Sharpes' buggy pulled in right behind them. No doubt, Alice had insisted they not lag too far behind, insuring that Byron act as the perfect gentleman. Vera had avoided talking to Alice about Byron since Wednesday night, but she wouldn't be able to hold off her sister's probing questions forever. The women knew each other well. Alice surely had sensed that something had happened between Byron and Vera. True, the fact that he mentioned kissing changed everything, showing Vera that Byron did harbor romantic notions about her. Her own response to the idea told Vera that her feelings for Byron had traversed onto new ground.

She didn't want the time with Byron to end. "Won't you join me for Sunday dinner?" she asked. "I baked a pudding for dessert."

"A pudding? What flavor?"

She twisted her lips into a wry grin. Surely he didn't care what flavor as long as they were in companionship. Realizing he was jesting, she shot back, "What flavor do you like?"

He shrugged. "Oh, let me see. Mango. Pineapple. Cricket."

"Oh, you!" She tapped him on the arm and laughed with more gusto than she had felt in some time. "If you want to wile away the afternoon with us, you'll have to settle on plain old vanilla and thank the Lord for it."

"Vanilla it is, then." Vera noticed that his gaze fixed on the Sharpes disembarking from their vehicle. "Are you sure your sister won't mind?"

"You are my guest, and I'll be doing my part in the dinner preparations, so there."

Byron chuckled. "You are getting bolder. I hope your family won't blame your high spirits on my influence."

"If they do, I'll thank them. It's about time I developed high spirits." She nodded once and took the hand he offered to help her descend from the carriage. His strong grip made her feel secure. Somehow, she knew that even if she tripped, his powerful arms would shield her from a fall.

Alice approached, holding the baby. "Thank you for escorting my sister to worship, Mr. Gates."

"My pleasure, Mrs. Sharpe."

"And you should be happy that I invited Mr. Gates to dine with us." Vera put on her most agreeable smile.

Elmer joined Alice. "You did? Good. It's about time you had Sunday dinner with us, Byron. We men can talk while the women fix dinner."

Byron grinned back. "Yes, I'm always primed for a good discussion concerning the news of the day."

Though Alice's demeanor indicated she wasn't thrilled with Byron's inclusion in their dinner plans, she didn't comment. Grateful, Vera confined her conversation to the contents of the sermon and the details of preparing the meal.

Over roast beef and mashed potatoes, Elmer kept Byron talking, and Vera appreciated that her sister refrained from saying anything unpleasant to their guest. Byron complimented every dish and raved over how smart little Paul already appeared. Vera could see by the way Alice's expression softened during those times that Byron's charms were working their wonders.

Vera knew Alice didn't want her to make a poor match, hence her reticence to accept Byron unabashedly. She prayed Alice would change her mind. At least Elmer was on her side, and Paul, in his innocence, smiled and gurgled at Byron. Vera enjoyed witnessing the connection Byron made with the youngest Sharpe. She sensed that Byron's magnetism could easily turn from attracting women to coaxing his children into obedience.

"Time to do the dishes, Vera," Alice said even before they partook of dessert.

"Oh, but I promised Byron some vanilla pudding." She suppressed a little laugh.

"Let me help you with the dishes, dear," Elmer offered.

"Thank you, Elmer." Vera made a mental note to do something nice for Elmer the next time the opportunity presented itself. "I'll dish up the pudding. Might we take dessert in the parlor?"

"Of course," Elmer said quickly. "Would you feel too put-upon if Alice and I had our dessert in the kitchen?"

In spite of mild objections and agreements whispered hastily by Alice to Elmer, Vera soon found herself alone in the parlor with Byron. She had brought in the pudding along with coffee on a tray and set the refreshments on the table. Alice and Elmer could be heard conversing in the kitchen.

"Seems like Alice and Elmer are having a good time. Maybe they're glad to get away from us," Byron joked. Just as quickly, his expression grew wistful. "Aren't they lucky to be so in love after all this time?"

"They haven't been married so very long. Only six years. But you're right. Love can expire long before that."

"I suppose not having the pressures of fast-paced modern city life can add to one's contentment." Byron took a taste of the promised vanilla pudding.

Vera froze in place, watching for his reaction to the dessert. To her delight, he shut his eyes and smiled dreamily.

"Mmm. That is some kind of good!" He looked at her and took another spoonful.

"Do you think I could please you if I baked a pudding every day?"

"Forever."

She caught something in his gaze that told her he was serious, but just as quickly the telltale light left his eyes, and he composed himself. Feeling a flush of mixed emotions, she hoped her own expression didn't reveal too much.

He cleared his throat. "On another topic, I've been observing you for a while now in a variety of situations. Will you let me in on a secret?"

"A secret?"

"Yes. You are so much at peace. Surely it isn't because you're so sheltered from the world?"

She felt her face grow hot. "I—I suppose I am what one would call sheltered. Surely much less worldly than the women you usually meet."

"You can trust me when I say that you compare most favorably to other women."

"Really?"

"Really. You need not seem so surprised." He paused. "Although I wonder if you wouldn't mind leaving your protected world for a trip now and again. You seemed so eager to hear about my travels when we last spoke."

Relieved that he had shifted the subject, she decided the best course of action was to begin a vigorous debate. "Yes, I do enjoy your stories of adventure."

He took a sip of coffee. "No doubt. Being a companion to a lady who remains in her bed at home most of the time as you were in Baltimore and now helping your sister here in the country—well, neither situation lends itself to adventure."

"Maybe not the type of adventure you consider. But my life is exciting enough for me. I am enthralled each day to see how Paul has grown, how much progress he is making. I see Alice and Elmer's happiness at the prospect of welcoming the new life she is carrying. I am thankful for the work I have to do, for the ability to read my Bible. In everything, I see the wonder of God's creation. That, I assure you, is more than enough excitement for me."

"So it is not excitement you seek in the traditional way but peace."

"Yes. Do you mind that terribly?"

"To my surprise, I don't."

She laughed. "I would still like to travel someday, although in the safety of modern conveyances. I'm not sure I'm one for an African safari or for climbing mountains in Switzerland."

"I've been on both types of expeditions, and though they were intriguing, I have no special desire to repeat them." Tasting his coffee, he seemed to ponder her words. "So where do you find your peace?"

"I was hoping it would be obvious that it is derived from my faith."

He didn't consider her question long. "Yes. I suppose it is."

"Nevertheless, I'm sorry you felt the need to ask. Am I such a poor ambassador for Christ?"

He set down his cup. "Indeed not! It is not your witness that is to blame for my obtuseness. Rather, it is my failure to see what is plainly in front of my face. Forgive me."

"Of course."

Relief evidenced itself in his small sigh. Then his expression tightened. "I hope you will continue to be so patient with me when I make my next confession."

"Confession?" Hadn't she heard enough bad revelations about Byron? What else could be left? She braced herself and forced her voice to sound strong. "What is it? You can tell me."

"Thank you for your confidence." He paused. "After some thought and prayer, and under duress, on Wednesday morning I'll be taking Clarence to Baltimore for a few days."

"Oh?" Though she tried to hold it back, she knew disappointment expressed itself upon her face.

"Yes," Byron answered. "I shall miss accompanying you to the midweek service."

"As will I. But I must ask, why are you taking Clarence to Baltimore at this time? Is there a particular reason?"

"It's to settle a wager."

"You made a bet with Clarence?"

"No, although he thinks I did, and he refuses to be convinced otherwise. I can see by his persistent references that he won't rest until one of us declares victory or defeat. So I have decided simply to treat him to a night on the town so I can be released of this perceived obligation."

"Knowing Clarence, I have no doubt he would resort to trickery to gain a night of entertainment."

Byron chuckled. "I must take the blame since my past caused Clarence to believe I would be eager to bet. I pray that the tentacles of my past are short ones and that I can soon embark on a trouble-free future. May I beg your indulgence and patience?"

"Of course. I will put my trust in the Lord that He will walk with you as you write the end of the dark chapters in your life. I will pray earnestly for that to happen, by your leave."

"Yes. Please do pray. I plan to resist temptation, but in the thick of it, one's resolve can weaken."

At that moment, Vera said a silent prayer that he would hold strong.

seven

An hour later when Byron went into the Stanley house, Clarence called out to him from his study. Byron joined him.

Clarence grinned at him from his usual chair and set down his paper. "Well, well, well. You're later than usual, old man. I had to dine alone. Does that mean Vera invited you in for dinner?"

He nodded as he took a seat.

"You don't seem as enthusiastic as a man should when he's making such fine progress. I thought she was nearly falling all over herself to get you accepted by her sister. What happened? Was Alice rude to you at dinner?"

"She wasn't too friendly, but I think she was beginning to warm up to me by meal's end."

"Ah, that old Gates charm. Why am I not surprised?" His face fell. "Uh oh. I suppose this means I'll be the one paying for the night on the town."

"Oh no, you won't. That's what I wanted to tell you. I know you won't rest until this idea of a bet is settled, and no matter how many times I tell you I have no intention of betting on my wooing of Vera, you insist we still have a wager."

"Now, am I as slippery as all that?" Clarence clucked his tongue.

"Worse."

Clarence laughed. "I suppose I am. So what is it you want to tell me?"

"To be rid of the idea you have of a wager, I want to offer you a night on the town in Baltimore and call it even."

Clarence joined the fingertips of both hands and touched his clean-shaven chin. "You're conceding? What a disappointment. Things are just getting interesting."

"Interesting for you, perhaps, but I desire nothing more than to rid myself of this albatross." Without thinking, Byron looked at his chest as if expecting to see a dead bird hanging from a rope around his neck.

"Have you no pride?" Clarence jested.

"Not anymore. At least not the type of pride that causes me to worry about losing and winning bets."

"All right, then. I'll be more than happy to spend a night out with you. I'll need a few days to settle matters here, and off we'll go."

"I thought as much, which is why I didn't plan to leave until Wednesday. I'll write and let Mother know we'll be staying at the house."

"Have you told her about your country mouse?"

"No." Byron flinched. The notion of telling Mother she could forget her dreams of Daisy as her daughter-in-law was not something he anticipated with glee.

"I wish I could be there to witness the day Vera Howard meets the formidable Mrs. Gates. I wonder how little Vera will seem beside the sophisticated Miss Estes?"

"They are a contrast, certainly. But Mother will come around. Once she realizes how Vera and I feel about one another and that Vera would make anyone a fine daughter-in-law—not to mention my wife—she'll be pleased."

"I still can't believe you've maintained any interest in Vera after all she's put you through."

"All she's put me through?"

Clarence shuddered. "That's right. Forcing you to sit through boring sermons and church socials, refusing to let you kiss her, and then acting as though she's better than you just because she can listen to the preacher drone for hours without her eyes glazing over. She should be on her knees thanking you for bringing some life into her boring existence. Before you came to visit, I assure you, she was the perfect little mouse. No man wanted her. And no other man ever will."

Byron felt the blood rise to his face. "I've decked men for lesser insults." He balled his right hand into a fist and punched it once in his open left palm.

Clarence blanched. "I beg your pardon. I suppose I didn't realize that this is not a game to you anymore. She's really gotten to you, hasn't she?"

"Yes," Byron admitted.

"And so quickly, too. I never thought I'd see the day." Clarence shook his head. "It's always hard to see a good man like you succumb."

"That's the problem. I'm not a good man. But I will be. You'll see."

ஒ

"Soup's wonderful," Elmer commented later over supper. The three were dining late, having already put the baby to bed for the night.

"I do believe it is every bit as good as the roast you served for dinner," Vera observed.

"Did you really taste it?" Alice added salt to her bowl of soup. "You seemed too interested in Mr. Gates to take in much of what you were eating."

"Yes, I'm surprised you even realized you ate roast," Elmer teased.

"Just barely. Although I am pleased that he enjoyed the pudding."

"Pudding. Yes," Alice remarked. "So just what did the two of you talk about while you were in the parlor?"

"Alice, can't you let them have a little privacy?" Elmer chided.

"When he admits he wants to court her and stops pussyfooting around, then they can have some privacy," Alice said.

Vera couldn't believe Alice even considered the possibility. "Are you saying you wouldn't mind?"

Alice gave a slight shrug. "He is charming, I must admit. But he hasn't won me over yet. Not completely, anyway."

Vera exchanged hopeful looks with Elmer.

"I worry," said Alice, "because he didn't seem to be in the best of spirits when he departed this afternoon."

"Oh. That." Vera hesitated. "Well, he's going to Baltimore for a spell, and I don't think he's happy about it."

"Doesn't want to leave you, eh?" Elmer ventured before drinking down his milk.

Vera's face flushed hotter than her soup. "I'd like to think that's part of the reason, but he isn't happy about why he's going."

"Not bad news, I hope," Elmer said.

Alice didn't echo his sentiment in words, but a concerned expression crossed her face, and she stopped eating.

"Not really. He has to take Clarence out for an evening."

"Oh, he has to, does he?" Alice's voice rose with suspicion. "If he's taking Clarence Stanley to Baltimore, that can only mean trouble."

"I'm aware that cities have a reputation for harboring evil, but that doesn't mean they will be doing anything wrong," Vera said.

"You know Clarence better than that. Even if Byron Gates's reputation were pure white, it's unlikely Clarence would be up to much good," Alice objected. "Did he tell you where they were going, or what their plans are?"

"No."

"Then I wouldn't trust either of them."

"Maybe you wouldn't, but I trust Byron," Vera said. "I think he is trying to change his ways and I'd like to give him the chance to show me that he means what he says."

"If you want my opinion, I think there's a chance he's putting on an act for you, Vera, and chasing other women behind your back," Alice said. "Why else would he develop this sudden need to go to Baltimore?"

"He could very well have some business to attend to while he's there," Elmer pointed out. "After all, his family still lives there, and that's where his family business is based."

"True, Elmer," Vera said. "I have no doubt he'll accomplish some business while he's there. And all will be well after he entertains Clarence this one night."

"So you would like to think," Alice noted. "I don't enjoy being cynical, but what if you're wrong?"

"Of course I wouldn't want to have a suitor court me if he's only putting on an act. But I have taken your advice to heart, Alice, even though you don't think I have been listening. I have been praying for discernment. I truly believe the Lord will show me if Byron proves false."

"Perhaps, but He also gave you an earthly sister to guide you. Vera, you should be grateful for a sister like me. I don't want to see you fall into the hands of a cad."

"Our Lord is a God of second chances. Even seven times. And seventy times seven. You don't seem to be willing to give Byron one."

"I appreciate your compassion, but you are too naïve to know what is best for you," Alice said. "With Mother and Father gone, you need our protection."

"Yes," Elmer agreed, "but only up to a point. After all, Vera lived on her own in Baltimore, and she conducted her affairs without reproach while she worked there."

Alice paused only momentarily. "I suppose you're right. I'm sorry, Vera. I really do mean well."

Vera nodded. "I know you do. And I'm grateful to have a sister who cares."

❧

That night, Byron wanted only to retire early, but Clarence was too excited by the prospect of the trip to sleep. He insisted that they engage in a game of chess.

Byron moved a knight and watched Clarence promptly capture the piece. "Good move."

"If only you concentrated on chess as much as you seem to be preoccupied with Vera Howard. I must confess, I am amazed by your persistence with her."

"Why is that? Am I a known quitter?" Byron moved a pawn.

Clarence studied the board and spoke without moving his eyes from a bishop. "No. But you are not known to change your ways for any woman. And while I must say I envy your fortitude in wanting to turn over a new leaf, do you think God would want your motive to be so you could capture a woman? It looks suspiciously like that's just what you might be doing."

"Is that so?" He watched Clarence make his next move.

"Yes." Clarence leaned back in his leather chair and crossed his arms.

Because the criticism came from a trusted friend, Byron took no offense. Rather, he contemplated the possibility while only halfway studying the chessboard. "Yes, I can see why it might appear that I'm not sincere in my motives. And you're right that no man should use God as a means to fulfill earthly desires. But I came here to visit you without knowing Vera at all. And I had already decided even before I boarded the train to come here that I wanted to seek a life that showed respect to God. No longer do I want a life of useless frivolity."

"And Vera has helped you stay on the new course."

"I don't deny that. Isn't the fact that she inspires me to her credit?" Byron moved a pawn, not caring whether or not the move would sacrifice the piece in short order.

"I suppose," Clarence conceded. "She always did impress me as the type more suited to a convent than a dance hall."

Byron looked to his friend. "She would consider that a compliment, although I know you don't mean it as such."

"Instead of letting those silly Baltimore debutantes discourage you, old man, why don't you seek a more adventurous type? Someone who's nothing like Vera. She doesn't fit your style."

He lifted his forefinger, mimicking a schoolmaster. "Correction. She didn't fit my style. But she does now."

"You've changed that much?" Clarence moved a pawn.

"I'd like to think so. And for good reason," Byron said. "It's not as though my former life was bringing me joy and comfort. Disgrace and disrespect was more like it."

"Maybe you should enter the ministry."

"Maybe that's the bet I should have taken instead of the one you offered."

"Ah, but ministers aren't supposed to be betting men."

"True, they are men of faith." Byron advanced another pawn even though he wasn't sure that was the best move.

Clarence captured the piece. "I'm surprised Vera has managed to hold your attention all this time. I must have underestimated her charm." He fingered the white pawn that was his prize and then set it back in its proper place in the wooden box from whence it came. "But I'm even more surprised by the way you seem determined to change your lifestyle and attitude. Why, it appears you truly can no longer concentrate properly on a simple chess match."

"I must let you win once in a great while," Byron responded. "After all, you have been kind to show me your hospitality all this time."

"Let me win indeed. Just for that, this will be the shortest, most devastating match on record." A mischievous glint that bordered on the vengeful entered Clarence's eyes.

Byron's lips contracted into a wry grin. "That's the spirit. Now the match will start to get interesting."

"Care to place a bet?"

"No." Byron didn't even let a hint of mischief or mirth color his voice. "No, I don't."

"Pity."

"I have much more important matters to occupy my mind."

Clarence's eyebrows shot up. "You mean, something—or someone—other than Vera Howard?"

"I sent a letter to my father about my intentions."

"Your intentions? Are you saying you intend to court Vera Howard?"

Byron captured a knight. "Regrettably, despite my success with Mrs. Sharpe today, I don't think I enjoy enough good standing to entertain such a prospect. At least not yet. No, it's about another change in my life. One that I think will please him indeed."

❧

The following day, Byron was surprised to receive not a letter but a wire from his father. The elder Mr. Gates was not known for extravagance, so the costly form of communication indicated the message contained a matter of import. As he read it, Byron's hands shook, an uncommon occurrence for one so confident.

Whereas Father had splurged on the telegram, the economy of words was evident. Yet they said enough: *Daisy Estes*.

eight

A few days later, as Byron readied himself to go to Baltimore, he tried to keep his mind off Daisy Estes. How could Father have come up with such an unfeeling response to his letter—her name appearing on an impersonal telegram?

When he heard a knock on the door to his room, Byron expected his visitor to be a maid bearing freshly laundered linens. "Come in."

"Sorry to disturb you, sir, but this just arrived." Clarence's valet handed him a letter bearing Father's precise handwriting.

Not surprised that Father chose to follow up his initial correspondence, Byron nodded and accepted the missive. He took a seat in the leather chair and waited for the valet to exit before he read it:

Byron,

I trust you received my wire and that the name Daisy Estes gave you pause as you waited, no doubt, for this letter to arrive. I realize you needed this time in the country to reflect upon your life. As you know, I am pleased that you have finally realized the time has come for you to throw off the ways of carefree bachelorhood to seek the more fulfilling rewards of marriage and eventual fatherhood. Not only is a man of your position expected to make such plans but also, indeed, to do so is his duty to God, country, and family.

While I am on the topic of religion, your mother was thrown into ecstasy by the news that you are seeking our

*Savior in a real way. Indeed, I was forced to retrieve the
smelling salts to prevent her from swooning. I trust the next
time you have news of such import to share that you will
caution your mother to remain seated.*

*But I digress. The Savior has blessed our lives with His
abiding presence, and you know that we believe Him to
be more than just a genie in a bottle to grant our wishes,
however worthy those wishes might be. I pray your spiritual
journey is not a trivial pastime for you but one that will
increase your richness of life.*

Byron paused in his reading and cringed. Father's observation, in its truth, hurt. He tapped the letter on the arm of
the chair before he resumed reading:

*Now as for richness of life, I have a word of caution for you
regarding this little diversion you have found for yourself in
the fresh country air. I am quite aware of and embarrassed
by the outcome of your most recent flirtation with Miss
Reynolds. Her rejection of you is widely known, though
I skirt the issue and provide nebulous answers just shy of
lying to protect what's left of your reputation whenever any
of our acquaintances hint of anything less than honorable.
I only pray your poor mother isn't exposed to stories of your
tomfoolery. Surely the refined ladies she befriends are either
unaware of your mischief or are too polite to inquire.*

*I can't help but wonder if the incident with Miss
Reynolds is at least part of the reason why you have taken
on this sudden and unexpected interest in religious matters.
Regardless of how He chooses to reach you, I shall not
complain.*

Yet I caution you not to confuse spiritual and physical

*matters. I implore you to remember that a flirtation with a
country mouse is all in good fun, but do remember that a fine
woman, Daisy, is here at home, waiting in the wings for you.
Rather than spurning her by carrying on out in the country,
you should be grateful her father is a friend of mine and that
the two of us—as well as your mothers—anticipate the joyous
day when our two families will unite through your marriage.*

*I hope and pray that you will reflect mightily upon the
content of this letter. I look forward to seeing you when you
arrive here in town this Wednesday.*

*Yours,
Father*

Despite the fact he was in danger of being overheard by
servants in the area, Byron let out a groan that reached all four
corners of his room. Perhaps he should have made things clear
as to where he stood with Daisy before he left town. Then
again, avoiding unpleasant situations and news had been part
of his old life—before Vera.

Flirting had seemed so amusing at the time, with both parties
exchanging flattering words that lifted the spirits. Harmless
trivialities, indeed. Or were they? Apparently not. Perhaps the
pastor of Vera's church was right. Coy words, empty promises
whispered under the moonlight were corrupt because they
could lead to carnal sin and emotional pain, both with long-
term consequences. When he first heard the sermon, Byron
thought the pastor was making much ado about nothing. But
now that Father's letter was in his hands, he could see that he
had created a most undesirable situation for all concerned. A
situation that was not going to resolve itself with ease.

He had to make amends. He knew how, but he didn't like
the prospect. If only he could find another way.

❧

Hearing the clomping of a horse's hooves on the dusty path leading to the Sharpe farmhouse, Vera kept her hands in the dough as she kneaded but still managed to get a peek.

She recognized the black horse with a star-shaped spot around his left eye as Byron's and knew that the man of whom she had grown fond had come for a visit. "Byron!"

Wishing she hadn't blurted his name, she scanned the portions of the dining room and hallway she could see through the open kitchen doors and sent up a prayer of thanks that she didn't see Alice, nor did she hear her sister protest Byron's approach. Alice, now well into her confinement, had taken on the habit of stealing an afternoon nap. Surely she and little Paul were both sleeping soundly. Elmer, out in the fields, would have little to protest in Byron's presence and was unlikely to leave his work this early.

Vera wiped her sticky hands clean on a damp cotton cloth and wondered if she should entertain a man with such a passive chaperone in the house, but to awaken Alice was taking a chance that, without Elmer's softening presence, her sister would encourage Byron to depart. And for him to make an appearance, Vera sensed he had something important to tell her.

Not willing to appear too eager, she busied herself with an imaginary spot on the counter until he knocked. As soon as he did, she rushed to greet him. "Byron. I didn't expect to see you again before you left for Baltimore. Is everything all right?"

He tipped his hat. "Vera, I beg your indulgence for my un-expected visit. I hope you will overlook my boldness and allow me a few moments with you?"

Did he really think he had to ask? She retained her composure. "Of course."

She realized the time had come to relocate since he still stood on the back stoop, hovering in the kitchen doorway. "Might I pour you a glass of lemonade? Perhaps we might sit out in the yard under the trees where it's cooler."

"That sounds like a fine idea to me." He looked past Vera into the house. "That is, if my presence won't offend your sister."

"She's asleep, and besides, I think you might have assuaged her heart a little the last time you were here. Especially since little Paul took to you so well." She decided not to repeat Alice's worries and speculations about Byron's trip to the city.

Respecting propriety, Byron waited on the porch while Vera made haste to pour lemonade. The couple then settled with their refreshments on stiff wicker chairs under a large oak tree with outstretched branches. For a few moments, they sat in companionable silence. A soft breeze blew against Vera's face. The air was welcome after her work in the hot kitchen all afternoon. She listened to the wind blowing through the leafy oak trees that dotted the yard.

The mixed-breed dogs, Spot and Peanut, inspected Byron and sniffed at his knees, asking for pats on the head before they ran off to romp on their own. Mouser, the cat who lived up to her name, took a well-earned nap on a vacant chair.

Having befriended the dogs, Byron stared off into the blue sky with its feathery white clouds. Was he trying to discern shapes in the cloud formations? She smiled at the thought that a grown man like Byron, so full of self-assurance, would be playing a boyish game. She sighed. Amid such peace, all felt right with the world. If only she could freeze the moment in time and enjoy it longer.

She discerned that such a wish was not to be as she watched Byron set his empty glass on the patch of lawn near the chair.

"Might I offer you another glass of lemonade?" she asked.

"Oh no, thank you, although the offer is tempting."

She looked at him. His words conveyed pleasantness, yet his facial expression had tensed. Obviously his visit involved more than letting her know he would be staying in the country a few more days, along with passing the time with refreshment and conversation. She wanted to ask what he was thinking but held back, sensing that he would reveal his meaning to her soon.

Byron's glass tipped to its side. Vera made no move to retrieve it since the grass had cushioned its fall. Byron didn't seem to notice the minor mishap. The obtuseness was unusual for him.

He cleared his throat. "Vera, I have something to tell you."

"Oh." She wished she could have uttered a more intelligent response, but anything she could say of any content would be groping in the dark. "Does your news have something to do with your trip?"

He nodded.

"You—you'll be returning soon?" She hoped her question didn't cause her to appear bold or, even worse, desperate.

Byron's expression didn't convey such an interpretation of her words. "Yes, that part of the plan hasn't changed. The visit will be brief."

She kept herself from breathing an audible sigh of relief. Curiosity piqued, she continued, "You'll be seeing your family, I assume. And all is well with them, I hope?"

He hesitated.

"Unless it's none of my concern," she rushed to apologize. "I didn't mean to pry. Forgive me."

"No, you're not prying. That's a perfectly sensible query. And yes, I will be returning to my childhood home. My parents inherited the townhome from my grandparents. I can't imagine it not being occupied by some of the Gates family."

"My family has been in this area for generations, as well. I know exactly what you mean."

"I do look forward to my visit with family. And of course, I have a few pressing business matters to attend to while I'm there. As you undoubtedly have learned, work takes no vacation."

She considered the batch of dough she had just prepared and remembered the other chores awaiting her. "How right you are. In that event, I wish you a wonderful visit and smooth resolution of your business affairs while you are in Baltimore."

"Thank you."

She perceived he had more to tell her. What could it be? She took the opportunity of silence to express her own thoughts. "I cannot tell you how gladdened I am that you stopped by today. You have offered me a most pleasant diversion."

"And you have done likewise for me."

Silence visited once more. She could feel the electricity between them. His feelings for her had grown. Though she had turned down his request before, now she longed for a kiss.

nine

Vera wondered if Byron felt the same. Did he want to kiss her as much as she yearned for him? She couldn't discern from his facial expression what he was thinking.

Alice's warning that Byron might be going to Baltimore to seek a sinful type of fun pulled at her mind. Vera didn't doubt that plenty of women in the city would enjoy his attentions. Yet he wasn't acting like a man in a hurry to visit another woman.

"I hope you don't mind my saying that I will miss you enormously while I'm away." Byron leaned toward her and looked into her eyes.

"No." Her voice was but a whisper, though his sentiment heartened her.

"Will you miss me just as much?" He sounded shy, somehow.

His vulnerability, uncharacteristic for Byron, emboldened her to take a chance. If he was toying with her, the response she gave would tell. If he had developed true feelings for her, she would learn that truth. She was ready for that certainty, whether it meant admitting Alice was right and putting all thoughts of Byron out of her mind once and for all, or if it meant she could think of spending her life forever with Byron.

"Yes. I will miss you terribly, too. Do say you'll be returning as soon as your business in Baltimore is complete."

Her throat constricted, and she became conscious of her beating heart. She searched his face for signs of his authentic feelings. His eyes widened, and the corners of his mouth turned upward, though not too much. No matter how cool he tried to portray himself, she could see in that instant that he yearned for her as much as she did for him.

"I dreamed of such a response. I couldn't leave without your assurances that I had not mistaken your communication during our last meeting—that you indeed want me to return."

"Yes." As soon as her admission left her lips, she realized how bold she sounded. An attack of shyness forced her gaze to the ground.

"Then, yes. I promise I will return as soon as my mission is accomplished."

There was something in the tone of his voice she didn't like. She sought to discern his hidden meaning. "Mission? I thought you were entertaining Clarence. But now you're making your trip sound more urgent. Is it?"

"I'm afraid it is." He hesitated.

Vera watched his body tense. He tightened his jaw. As she waited for him to speak, Vera's thoughts ran wild. He said his family was doing well, so apparently no close relative suffered from an illness. But what about Byron himself? Had he developed odd physical symptoms that were causing him to seek a doctor's advice?

"Are you ill?" she blurted out.

A stunned look crossed his face. "Ill? But no." He pursed his lips. "Please forgive my lack of attention. What I have to say is not easy."

"Whatever it is, I will do my best to understand." She waited for him to enlighten her.

He hesitated.

Her mind played out another scenario. He had mentioned business. Was his family concern in trouble—a turn of events he didn't want to admit? Did he think he would be less desirable in her eyes if his business had fallen upon hard times?

"If your troubles are financial, please know that I only ask the Lord each day for enough."

"As the Lord's Prayer instructs us."

She nodded.

"I admire your attitude about money, Vera. Many women do not share your philosophy. But I can assure you, money is not my worry."

"Then do tell me," she begged. "My mind has already filled with too many unthinkable possibilities. Whatever do you mean by your mission?"

"I—I must visit a lady of my acquaintance."

Vera stiffened. "A lady?" Alice had never missed an opportunity to warn her that Byron had unfinished business with a number of women, so why was she surprised? She forced herself to remember that at least he trusted her enough to be honest. A lesser man would have hidden his reason for going to the city. "You're planning to visit a lady?"

"Yes. A nice, respectable lady. A lady who both of our families hope will join me in marriage."

Vera gasped. "Oh." She couldn't remember a time she had felt more distress, but she didn't dare express it. She had already made a fool of herself as it was. Her humiliation was such that at that moment she would have welcomed Alice's appearance to interrupt this conversation, even if she were bearing her most stern look and admonition.

Vera straightened herself in her chair. "You are a free man. You do not need my permission to see anyone you wish. I hope your visit with her is all you anticipate it will be." Had Vera been a woman of demonstrable emotions, she would have burst into tears, her voice quivering. But having been reared to be strong, she was able to maintain her composure. "So you are. . . promised. . .to this woman?"

Please, Lord, don't let it be so!

Byron wasted no time in consoling her. "No. Please don't think that. If I were, I never would have pursued any type of relationship with you. Unfortunately for our parents, neither the lady nor I wish to marry. At least, not each other."

Surprise, relief, and confusion reared their heads, leaving her in turmoil. "What? I'm afraid I still fail to understand."

"She has already told me that she has another beau who's been pursuing her."

"And that doesn't bother you?"

"Not in the least."

Not in the least. When had Vera heard four more lovely words? She couldn't recall. "Well, it's settled then, isn't it? You and she have agreed to part ways." Her voice sounded too hopeful, reflecting the unwelcome jealousy she felt.

"There were no ways to part. At least, not as far as I'm concerned."

"Really? Then how could your parents have come to the conclusion that the two of you were betrothed?" She paused. "I'm sorry. I'm not passing judgment. I'm trying to make sense of what you're saying."

"And rightfully so. If I am going to live my life as an honest man of integrity, as I hope to do from now into the future, I must be truthful in all of my dealings. Thank you, by your sweet spirit, devotion, and example, for encouraging me to that end." He sat back in his chair but didn't look at her. "I am putting myself at risk of sounding ungentlemanly by saying this, so please keep it in confidence. I'll begin by saying that I've known Daisy since we were children."

Vera didn't speak but held back her disdain. The fact that her rival had a name didn't ease her mind at all. She wished she hadn't heard the name. Vera concentrated on the fact that

Byron was taking her into his confidence and kept listening.

"Our mothers thought we looked cute together when we were little, so they thought it would be a fine idea if one day we were to wed. No one paid attention to their plans. Even when we were older, both of us assumed our mothers would realize their fantasies were just that—idle dreams. We were sure once we made our intentions known to others, all plans would be forgotten. But they weren't."

"So you and Daisy never had romantic attachments?"

"Nothing beyond some unfortunate flirtations now and again. Neither of us took them seriously."

"Women are tenderhearted, Byron. Suppose Daisy did take you seriously?"

"But she didn't. I know her." His lips thinned into a serious line before he resumed his explanation. "Daisy has a good reputation, yet she is a flirt, often inviting the attentions of men. She is just as quick as any man to offer a flattering phrase or two."

"Oh!" Vera wondered how unsophisticated she must seem when Byron remembered Daisy. She tried not to wince.

"So you can see why Daisy is not for me. I would prefer someone. . .someone more reserved." He looked into her eyes. "Someone like you."

Vera didn't know what to say. She returned his feelings and wanted to admit it, but the words wouldn't leave her lips. She couldn't remember a time when she had been sorry that her mother had reared her to act in the reserved manner of a true lady. Her training had become so ingrained that she found it impossible to be bold at such a moment. When Byron spoke, dissolving her need to respond, she felt grateful.

"I trust you will keep this confidence to yourself." The tone of his voice indicated he didn't doubt she would.

"Of course. But did you love her at one time?" Almost afraid of the answer, she kept her voice to whisper.

"No, I did not. Not in a romantic way, as you mean it. And as I said, any silly flirtations between us are now firmly affixed in the past. Daisy, unlike my family, understood that no binding promises were ever made. At least, that is my impression. Our families—our fathers got in on the act once they learned of our mothers' enthusiasm—were the ones who jumped to the conclusions, painting the picture they wanted to see.

"So you must understand that it's not Daisy who concerns me, but my family. I simply feel that I must go to her and be absolutely sure that all parties are freed from any expectations whatsoever of our future together. This is not something I feel I should do by letter. This type of errand is better performed in person, even though the urge to take the coward's way out and resolve the matter by missive has crossed my mind more than once."

Sympathy for Byron filled her. "I am glad you are no longer a coward."

His returning smile looked wry. "You are certainly refreshing, Miss Vera Howard."

"Really? What did you expect me to say?"

"I don't know. I suppose some women would have screamed. Some would have cried. Others would have refused to see me again. One or two might have thrown a glass of lemonade in my face."

"My, but you do sound as though you've been through more than one incident involving women." She kept her voice teasing, but the question underneath was serious.

"Being the coward that I was, I kept unpleasant confrontations to a minimum. That is why I face this situation now." He smiled. "And I do thank you for not throwing lemonade at me."

"I prefer to drink it. Besides, I do especially like that suit you're wearing."

They laughed. Their shared humor only heightened their increasing bond.

ten

Moments later, Vera managed to reenter the house without disturbing Alice. Examination of the waiting dough proved it was ready to be formed into rolls. She punched it down, then pulled the elastic ball from the bowl and, after flouring a space on the kitchen counter, began her task. Absorbed in her work, Vera hardly noticed when Alice emerged from her nap.

"Did I hear voices earlier, or was I dreaming?" Alice asked as she passed the threshold from the hall to the kitchen.

Vera hesitated but kept working the dough. "Byron dropped by."

"Byron?" Alice went for the teakettle. "I thought he was in Baltimore."

"Not yet. He soon will be. I served him a glass of lemonade in the backyard. I assure you: All was proper."

Vera waited for Alice to pry, but she seemed satisfied with the news that Byron would be gone for some length of time.

"Would you like some help?" Alice nodded toward the batch of dough.

"Certainly."

The two women sat at the kitchen table, breaking off pieces of dough, shaping them into round forms, and folding them in half to form what they liked to call "pocketbook" rolls since the resulting shape looked much like a lady's purse.

Since they saw each other every day and had no fresh news, the sisters worked in silence. The stillness gave Vera time to meditate on the afternoon. She and Byron had parted with easy banter, but her heart suffered from weightiness now that he had left. Her worst nightmares had come true. Byron had admitted that both sets of parents were expecting a marriage. What if they pressured Byron and Daisy to change their minds once Byron got to Baltimore? Even worse, what if Byron was mistaken, and Daisy really did expect them to wed? Then she would be convinced, and the two families could make Byron feel obligated to wed Daisy. But since Byron had recently renewed his commitment to Christ, would he be more malleable and feel he must go along with their wishes for marriage?

A terrible thought visited her. If something went awry, and Byron and Daisy were convinced to change their minds, Vera could lose Byron forever!

Lord, I pray for Thy will, whether it be for Byron to remain in Baltimore and abide by his family's wishes or to return here. Thou knowest best. In Jesus' precious name, amen.

The prayer brought Vera a realization. She had not prayed either for her own happiness or for Byron to be convinced to follow the path that she would have him follow. Her feelings were true.

Without a doubt, she had fallen in love with Byron Gates.

❧

Wednesday afternoon, Byron and Clarence arrived in the city via an eastbound B&O Railroad passenger car.

"Look alive, old man." Though he prodded Byron, Clarence looked out the hired carriage window and observed the streets of Baltimore. "Ah, the hustle and bustle of people going places and doing important things. Not like that backwater place we came from." He leaned forward and rubbed his palms together, bringing to Byron's mind how a starving man might anticipate a Thanksgiving Day feast. "We're finally in the city where we both belong."

"Yes," Byron answered despite wishing he were still in the country.

"You seem sullen, old man. Aren't you looking forward to our night on the town?"

Byron wasn't sure how he wanted to answer.

"Now look here," Clarence persisted. "You promised me an evening of merriment, and there's nothing you can do to squirm your way out of it. I'm surprised you'd even try." He patted Byron on the shoulder. "You'll liven up when you get to the gaming tables. I'm sure of it."

"You're assuming I plan to take a few turns, but I don't."

Clarence's expression fell. "Certainly you don't plan to spoil my fun."

"No. I simply don't have any intention of playing any games myself, that's all. But don't despair. You're sure to find many new friends to share in your idea of fun."

At that moment, the carriage passed the Estes residence, a fine brick townhome with four windows across the second-story front. "I know why you're in such a dejected mood. You don't want to see Daisy."

Byron looked at the house, glad that no one stood outside to note his arrival in town. He would see Daisy in his own time and not a moment sooner. "Actually, I do. I need to put this ridiculous matter of a marriage to rest once and for all. It's my mother I hate to disappoint."

For once, Clarence turned serious. "I don't blame you for feeling that way. No man, not even a scoundrel such as myself, wants to disappoint his mother. But your dear mama will recover. Mothers have a way of forgiving their sons no matter what the cost."

Byron chuckled. "You should know," he said in jest.

They turned into the gateway of Byron's childhood home,

which, with its well-tended yard and abbreviated porch, looked much like the Estes family's house in style and bearing.

The butler had barely greeted them before Mrs. Gates, who bore the same blue eyes as Byron, rushed to embrace him. "Oh, my darling son, I've missed you so."

"And I missed you, Mother."

She took him by both forearms and gazed into his face. "Let me look at you."

"Mother, I've only been away a few weeks, not ten years." He chuckled.

"Oh, but it feels like ten years. Maybe longer." She inspected him from head to toe. "Well. Strikingly handsome as always." She nodded to Clarence. "I see you've been taking good care of him out there in the country."

Clarence nodded. "I've been trying."

Mother motioned for them to follow her into the parlor. "I've already told Mattie to bring in tea. Now tell me all about the country, Byron. How many hearts have you broken?"

"At least one," Clarence said.

Byron's mother kept her attention on her son. "Only one? You must indeed be settling in to the idea of the wedding. When are you and Daisy going to set a date? Oh, please say you're finally ready. Her mother and I want to start planning the bridal dinner and reception."

"Don't schedule the caterer yet, Mother."

"Oh, why not, Byron?" Clarence teased.

Byron shot him a dirty look, and Clarence snickered. Byron's mother looked at them both indulgently, as though the two grown men were nothing more than mischievous, albeit charming, little boys.

Byron couldn't remember an afternoon when he had looked forward to teatime less.

eleven

The following day, the Esteses' butler took some time to respond to Byron's knock even though Daisy always kept Thursday afternoons open to greet callers. Byron could only hope she hadn't become indisposed, given how much he didn't want to have to gather up the courage to make the approach to her house a second time.

He was about to rap on the door once more when it finally opened. The butler greeted him as warmly as a proper butler permitted himself, and Daisy, thankfully, didn't keep him waiting long.

She entered the formal parlor on a cloud of pink, her usual color and her dress stylish as always, and greeted him with an embrace. "Why, Byron, I thought you had fled to the country to get away from the city heat." She took a seat on a red velvet divan. Her motion allowed Byron to sit in a matching chair across from her.

"Yes, it's cooler there. I'd forgotten how hot it can get here, even in June."

"Indeed," she concurred. "In fact, you're lucky to catch me today. I just returned from New Hampshire, and I'll be on my way to my cousin's in Rhode Island in three days. Much cooler weather in both locales, I must say. Oh, speaking of cooling off, might I offer you a drink?"

"No, thank you. I just had refreshment at home."

"That's too bad. Cook just baked some tarts, and I know how much you love those. Won't you reconsider?"

81

"If only I could."

"Have your way, then," Daisy said.

"Might I inquire after your dear mother?"

"She's as usual. All in a tither over what to pack for our visit to Rhode Island. I say, just take everything!" She giggled. "Ah, I'll be glad to have the packing behind us so we can escape. So how are things in the country?"

"Quite pleasant."

"And Clarence?"

"He is in fine form."

"No doubt. Well then," she said, "what brings you back so soon?"

"You do, in fact."

"I do? Oh dear." She put on a blush Byron was sure she must have practiced in the mirror. "Am I as memorable as all that?"

"Of course you are memorable." He bit his tongue. He hadn't been with Daisy for any amount of time, and already, he had slipped down the slope of flirtation. Fallen right into the abyss, rather.

"You are the flatterer as always," she said, confirming just how deeply he had sunk.

He put on a serious expression. "I am here to set the record straight. About us."

"Us?" She flicked her hand. "Is there an us?"

"I think you know the answer to that. My mother greeted me upon my arrival with probing questions regarding our impending wedding date."

To his surprise, Daisy's cheeks turned white.

"What's the matter, Daisy?"

"I know our mothers have been conniving and scheming, but I've been doing my best to discourage them. Well, I've been trying to discourage my mother, anyway." She sent him a fearful look. "You. . .you didn't think. . ."

"No. No, I didn't." Then, realizing he sounded as though he were rejecting her, he rushed to add, "Not that any man wouldn't be honored to marry you."

Daisy let out a laugh. "This is the reason why you stay in trouble, Byron. You don't know how to keep your lips from spilling words as smooth as glass. No wonder all the women in Baltimore wish they could be by your side. All except Elizabeth Reynolds. And maybe a few others whose hearts you've broken over the years." She shot him a wry look.

He groaned. "Must everyone in Baltimore know about my follies?"

"The summer drags on, and people do talk." She leaned closer. "I wouldn't waste time worrying about those silly debutantes if I were in your position. Elizabeth in particular really isn't up to your standards. She's much too thin and such an awful nose! Why you even flirted with her, I'll never know."

Her comments took him back to the time when Clarence insisted that Vera wasn't his type. What was it about him that invited such speculation? He decided to pursue another, more interesting angle. "Since everyone is gossiping about me, am I to presume that they believe you to be nursing your wounds?"

She only missed a beat. "Oh, you mean does everyone think you cheated on poor little me?"

A pang of chagrin visited Byron. "Is that how you feel? That I cheated?"

She laughed. "Indeed not! I've known you since we were children, Byron. And I know our mothers and their plans. We are both pawns in their dreams, even though no doubt they want what's best for us."

"And our families."

"Yes, that, too." She swallowed. "And now it's my turn to say that any woman would be fortunate to land you. You have it all: charm, good looks, a fine family name, and wealth."

"Then why aren't you chomping at the bit to take your place in line?" he jested in spite of himself.

"You know as well as I do. Because we're more like brother and sister than romantic mates. We'll always be the best of friends. But lovers? I know you too well for that." She crossed her arms and sent him a mischievous smile that reminded him of the time when they were but six and eight and had taken penny candy from Mr. Ashe's corner store.

"Should I be relieved or insulted?" The rhetorical question parted from his lips before he remembered to practice discretion.

She laughed. "Whatever you feel, you feel. But resist any urge to think I have insulted you. I wouldn't dream of it. I'm much too fond of you."

"And I, you."

"Good. Now that we have that all settled, which one of us will break the news to our mothers and clear the air once and for all?"

Byron didn't bother to conceal his distress. "I suppose you'll have to set your mother straight, and I'll have to talk to mine. Not a prospect I relish."

"Perhaps you can console her with the news that you have found an enchanting companion out in the country. No doubt, her cheeks are as ruddy as fall apples, and her skin is as creamy and white as the milk she gathers from the cows each morning."

Byron shook his head. "Why do I sense that your tongue lies firmly in your cheek?"

"Because it does. Really, Byron, will you be happy forever and ever with a naïve little thing from the country?"

"She's not naïve. And how do you know about Vera, anyway?" Byron asked.

Daisy crossed her legs. "So that's her name. A blond, I hear?"

"You hear correctly. But from whom?"

She smiled. "Clarence wrote to James, and he told Edna, and she told yours truly."

"The gossip mill is always grinding, I see."

"Of course. You are ever so interesting, and everyone wants to know all about your doings." She sat back on the divan as though she were about ready to take in a show.

"So you say. Why anyone would be interested in someone they think to be a cheater, I'll never know."

"It's because you dare to do the things that no one else does. That's part of your charm."

"It won't be for much longer. Since visiting the country, I have become more spiritual."

She covered her lips with both hands to suppress a hearty laugh. "You? Spiritual? The only spirits I know of associated with you are port wine and cognac."

The truth stung. Viewing himself through the loving though unflinching lens of an old friend—a compassionate female rather than his reckless friend Clarence—showed him all the more why he had to change and make that change permanent. "Not anymore."

"Really?" She shrugged. "Well then, we broke our make-believe engagement just in time. I wish you luck in your journey."

"And your journey? What do you believe the future holds for you?"

"It is quite promising, thanks partly to you."

"To me?" he asked.

"Yes. The rumor that you were unfaithful sent me quite a

few new prospects. I must remember to thank you. So thank you." Her face flashed naughtiness.

"Why would you care about new prospects? You told me yourself that Horace Moore was your intended beau."

She waved her hand. "Oh, he's yesterday's news." Her face turned serious. "I'll have you to know that Silas Jenkins was among those new prospects."

An image of a short man who was attractive enough but full of bluster entered his head. "Silas Jenkins? Surely you jest."

"You mean because he's not yet in our social set? He will be, I assure you. He certainly has the money to socialize with us."

"Money doesn't buy respectability."

"Maybe not, but having more than enough makes life a lot more fun, doesn't it?"

"Money aside, Jenkins has displayed quite a bit of nerve to make a play for a woman as far out of his league as you."

Both of her eyebrows rose. "Jealous words coming from a man who just broke off our so-called betrothal."

"Not jealous, Daisy," he said. "I will always care about you. I would like to see you make a good marriage. And so will your father. You jested about my country companion, but I doubt the prospect of you making a match with Jenkins will give your family much consolation."

She pouted. "I know. Daddy has already told me he doesn't approve. But my heart has spoken to me, Byron. And now and forever more, Silas's name is etched upon it."

Byron studied her eyes. All sauciness had vanished, replaced by raw emotion. "He is blessed to have garnered your favor. I mean that."

"So you wish me well?" Her wide eyes and voice drained of teasing told him that his approval was important to her.

"Of course I do, although I don't envy you for having to face your father."

"Silas will be by my side, and together, we can face anything."

"Spoken like a true romantic."

"A true romantic who's afraid," she admitted.

"I can understand that. Disappointing one's parents is never desirable, but we must be free to make our own decisions." He thought for a moment. "Shall we pray about the situation?"

Her palm dropped on the arm of the chair with such force that it banged on impact. "Pray? What good will that do?"

"I don't know. But maybe God will listen and will speak to your father's heart."

Her expression softened. "You really do mean what you said about this spiritual quest, don't you?"

He nodded.

"I'm sorry, then, that I made fun of you."

"Based on what you know about me, I deserved it. So will you pray with me?"

She paused. "I don't suppose it can hurt."

Byron bowed his head and spoke. "Father in heaven, please guide Daisy in Thy will for her life. We don't know what the future holds. Only Thou knowest. Whatever Thy plans are, let her and her future husband walk by Thy side. Keep them under Thy guidance and protection all of their days. In the name of Jesus, amen."

She looked up and studied him. "That was the oddest prayer I ever heard. Why didn't you ask God to make my parents understand us and accept Silas?"

"Because that may not be what is best for you."

"I thought you were on my side."

"I am. That's why I prayed for God's best. I hope in my heart that His plan coincides with what you want. But sometimes what we think we want can be the worst possible outcome for us."

Daisy shook her head as though she had just heard an incomprehensible university lecture. "I don't know, Byron. Maybe you shouldn't pray for me anymore." Her tone displayed more uncertainty than judgment.

"I won't pray for you if you prefer that I not. But I hope you really don't feel that way. I pray this way now because I am putting my trust in God as my heavenly Father, not as my errand boy."

She took a moment to digest what he said. "I can see what you mean. So who has been influencing the way you look at God now?"

Byron didn't hesitate. "The person you think to be a little ruddy-cheeked milkmaid. Miss Vera Howard."

twelve

Moments later, a free man, Byron whistled as he made his way across the generous foyer of the Estes home. He crossed the threshold, his waiting horse in sight.

Rolling his glance to the sidewalk, he slowed his pace when he realized that someone else awaited, too.

Daisy's father.

The large fellow, dressed in the suit he had worn during his day of toil in the office, lumbered toward him, a smile covering his countenance.

"Byron!" he boomed when he caught up to him on the porch steps. "There you are, my boy. I was wondering how long it would take for you to show your handsome mug around here."

Byron tipped his hat. "Good afternoon, Mr. Estes."

Mr. Estes drew closer. "Have you seen Daisy?"

"Yes, sir. She's looking lovely as usual."

"Of course she is! Now do my eyes deceive me, or does it look like you're trying to make a beeline for the street?" the older man queried.

"I'm due home for dinner soon."

"Nonsense! You're having dinner with us."

"Thank you, sir, but not this evening—"

"What's the matter? A big slab of roast beef isn't good enough for you anymore?" He let out a laugh as hearty as the portion of meat he suggested.

"Oh no, roast beef sounds delicious."

"Well then, there's no reason for you not to stay—if you

can stand all the talk that's bound to be happening about the wedding. My womenfolk do like to chatter."

"About that—"

He slapped Byron on the back. "I know, I know. But women get excited about these things. After dinner we can sneak into the library for a nice glass of port, eh?"

"Really, I can't." Byron looked toward the street.

Daisy's father tugged Byron's sleeve, leading him into the house. "If you're worried about your mother, I'll have Lester send word." He called out Lester's name.

"Please. Don't. I really, really can't stay."

Mr. Estes's face took on an expression of regret. "So you honestly do have plans for this evening? Tomorrow night, then."

"No, not tomorrow night, either."

Daisy joined them. "Daddy. I thought I heard you."

He hugged Daisy with one arm. "My little muffin. How was your day? Wonderful, I'm sure, now that your intended is back from the country."

Byron sent Daisy a look. She shot one back. In spite of his reluctance, he knew the time had come to set things straight once and for all with the Estes family. Surely Daisy's father would take disappointment better with Byron present rather than Silas.

"What's this?" Mr. Estes asked. "Do I sense a little tension in the air? A lovers' spat? Well, you have all evening to make amends. This, too, shall pass."

"No, Daddy, we didn't have a spat. Byron and I are still the best of friends."

"More than friends, I hope."

"Daddy, please come with us and sit in the parlor." Daisy's mouth was set in a firm line.

Her father looked at them both quizzically but complied. Byron sent Daisy an approving, if worried, look. The idea of being sure her father was seated when he heard the news seemed like a good one.

"So what is this about?" Mr. Estes inquired from the comfort of the settee. "Is there some detail about the big day that's distressing you? You know I said you can have anything you want."

"No matter what man she marries?" Byron asked.

Mr. Estes snapped his head toward Byron. "I beg your pardon?"

Daisy cleared her throat. "That's right, Daddy. Will you give me a nice wedding no matter whom I marry?"

He returned his attention to his daughter. "Don't be ridiculous. That's not even an issue. You're marrying Byron. Our two families have been planning this day for years."

"Did you hear yourself?" Daisy asked. "You said our two families have been planning. But you didn't mention the bride and groom."

"What are you saying?" All color left his face, soon to be replaced by a brilliant shade of red.

Byron braced himself. "Daisy is a beautiful woman. A remarkable woman. I suppose that's why I was always reluctant to speak up in opposition to our marriage."

He stood. "You. . .you are opposed to wedding my daughter?" Rage covered his face.

"And I am opposed to marrying Byron," Daisy jumped in, much to Byron's relief.

"Why?" Mr. Estes snapped. "I picked Byron for you."

"That's right, Daddy. You did. And he's a wonderful— friend."

"Good marriages begin with friendship."

Daisy set a comforting hand on his forearm. "If the friendship sparks into romantic feelings. And though, to please you, we have tried for years, all Byron and I have come up with are wet matches."

"A colorful but true analogy," Byron agreed, standing. "I love Daisy like a sister. As much as I don't want to disappoint you—and I know she doesn't want to disappoint you either—we simply cannot go through with the marriage you and my parents have planned for us. I'm sorry, Mr. Estes. I respect you almost as much as my own father, and I regret that I can't deliver the news you desire."

"Me, too, Daddy."

Mr. Estes thought for a moment, but his anger seemed only to increase. "I think I know what this is about. It's about that little country tart, isn't it? I know all about her."

"Country tart?" Byron fought two emotions: the urge to slug the man for referring to his godly Vera in such a derogatory manner, and the impulse to laugh out loud at the preposterous designation which revealed that Mr. Estes didn't know the first thing about Vera.

"No, Daddy, this woman is not what you call a tart," Daisy insisted. "I've been talking with Byron, and I can see that she has changed him. Why, he even prayed with me."

Mr. Estes narrowed his eyes at Byron. "What? You've decided to become a monk now to get out of your obligation to Daisy?"

"No, sir—"

"Daddy, it's not that way at all!"

Though he tried to maintain a brave facade, Byron shook inside. Daisy's father put on a good show, but Byron always knew that Mr. Estes desired him as a son-in-law not because of his person but because of his family's position and wealth.

The man who planned to be his father-in-law looked upon the marriage as a union of two families.

Daisy tried to calm her father. "Don't blame him. I have found someone else, too."

His expression tightened and a vein in his forehead developed sudden prominence. "Who? And why didn't I know about this?"

"Would you have listened?"

Mr. Estes stiffened his jaw. "Who is it?"

Daisy opened her mouth, but Byron didn't hear any words. He could only help Daisy by spitting it out himself. "Silas Jenkins."

Mr. Estes's eyes widened. "Silas Jenkins? Why, he is a nothing!" Rage returned to his face.

Byron cringed upon hearing any human being called a nothing. His regard for the man diminished by the second.

Mr. Estes pointed his finger at them. "I will not stand for this. Do you hear me? I will not stand for it! Byron, you will not divorce yourself of this obligation. You will not be a party to disappointing my wife, who has wanted this for both of you ever since I can remember. You and Daisy will be married by this time next year."

Daisy intervened. "Please, don't force us."

"You are my daughter, and you'll do as I say."

"But you can't make Byron—"

"Oh, can't I?" His gaze bored into Byron. "You will do as I say. Your family is powerful, but so is mine. I have overlooked the rumors, the gossip, the shenanigans. You thought I never was the wiser, didn't you? Well, I know all about you. I'm not surprised you tried to pull such a stunt. But you won't get away with it. You will keep your word, or I will ruin your reputation even more than it already is and undercut your family's business.

Don't think I won't make good on my promise."

Byron could see that Mr. Estes was serious, and he could also see there was no way out. He looked at Daisy, who sent him a helpless look before she ran out of the room in tears.

"See what you've done?" Mr. Estes said.

"See what I've done? Don't you care about your own daughter's happiness?"

"Her mother and I weren't in love on the day we wed, yet our marriage is very successful. You and Daisy will grow to love one another just as Mrs. Estes and I have."

"I beg your pardon, but the twentieth century has arrived and, with it, new attitudes about love. Attitudes that I believe will make for even stronger unions."

Mr. Estes huffed. "I beg your pardon!"

Seeing nothing to be gained by incensing the older man further, Byron acquiesced. "I beg your forgiveness for any disruption I have caused here today, sir. I never meant for this to happen."

Mr. Estes nodded curtly. "Then prove it. You have two weeks to get your affairs in order, Mr. Gates. After that time, I expect you to return here, hat in hand, prepared to set a date with my daughter."

thirteen

That evening, Byron managed to put on a good front during dinner at his house. After all, Mother had instructed Cook to prepare his favorite chicken dinner, and Byron wanted Clarence to enjoy his stay. He intended to relish the treat unhindered by thoughts about how he was going to make Vera his bride while maintaining the friendship—or at least avoiding adversarial relationships—between the Estes and Gates families.

"Cook has outdone herself," he told his mother.

"I would agree, my boy," Father said.

"I would hope this might be a celebratory dinner," Mother said. "I understand you went to Daisy's today."

Her observation caught him with a piece of meat in his mouth. He choked slightly.

Father rose and deposited several hits to his back. "There, there, my boy. Marriage is a frightening prospect, but your mother and I did just fine."

Byron's choking spasm passed. "I know, Father. You two did more than fine. But you were blessed to find a woman as remarkable as Mother."

"Agreed," Clarence offered.

"You are too kind." Mother smiled sweetly and patted her lips with her napkin. "So, have you and Daisy finally set that date?"

Byron knew the confusion he felt showed on his face. He turned to Father. "You. . .you didn't show her the letter?"

"What letter?" Mother wanted to know.

Father rushed to answer. "He wrote me some foolishness about meeting someone in the country and wanted to know what I thought. I reminded him about Daisy. I thought that settled it." He stared down his nose at Byron. "You failed to understand me?"

"No, sir, but Daisy is not interested in me, nor am I in her," Byron admitted. "I wish I could give you the news you want to hear, but I couldn't even if I had never laid eyes on Vera Howard."

"Oh, surely she's just getting a case of bridal jitters," Mother said. "That will change in the excitement of the parties and prenuptial events."

"No, it won't," Byron told her, though he kept his tone respectful. "Daisy told me today she is intrigued by Silas Jenkins."

"Silas Jenkins?" Father spat out his name. "You shouldn't let him scare you into taking a woman out in the country. You should be able to overcome any competition from him in the blink of an eye. Are you game?"

"No, sir."

"What's that you say?" Father set down his fork, and his voice donned an uncomfortable edge.

Byron strengthened his voice but continued to make a point of not taking on a disrespectful tone. "No, sir."

Mother's china coffee cup rattled as she set it down with too much force against the saucer. "Oh, Jack, I knew we shouldn't have let Byron wander away from home by himself." A tear rolled down her cheek.

Byron pursed his lips to keep from reminding his mother that he had celebrated his fifth birthday two decades in the past.

"So you have given up on Daisy?" Father asked.

"Yes, sir. But as I said, Daisy's heart is not broken. Neither is mine."

Clarence piped up, "Why, I wouldn't be surprised if Jenkins doesn't ask Byron here to be his best man."

Sobbing, Mother rose from the table and fled the room without excusing herself.

"Not again," Byron moaned under his breath.

An embarrassed grimace covered Clarence's countenance as he addressed Byron's father. "I'm so sorry, sir. I was only trying to lighten the atmosphere."

Father threw his napkin over his food. "I just lost my appetite."

"Please, Father. Understand. Vera Howard is a lovely girl. You would proud to have her as a daughter-in-law." He looked at Clarence from the corner of his eye and noticed that his friend was putting on a good show of composing his features into an unreadable expression.

Apparently Father must have caught Byron's furtive glance. "Clarence, what do you think of this girl?"

"Uh—um—"

"Spit it out, Clarence."

"I've known her since we were both children. She is a petite blond with not a whiff of scandal to her name, and her family is highly respected."

"If you don't believe Clarence, ask Raleigh Alden," Byron added. "Miss Howard was Mrs. Alden's companion for a time. She was like one of the family."

"A paid companion? Never let it be said that I look down on working people, but I had thought you would wed someone of breeding. Someone of our class."

"I know, but though Miss Howard isn't in our social set, she is far above many who are. Her character is beyond reproach.

She has helped me to become a better man. I believe that if she does consent to let me court her, that you and mother will be charmed by her refined manners and reserve once you meet her. Did I mention she's presently helping her sister with her new baby? Mother should like the prospect of a good mother for her future grandchildren."

Mr. Gates looked at his son's friend. "And you confirm this assessment, Clarence? Don't give me any coy answer. I am serious."

"Yes, sir. Everything Byron says is true. Miss Howard does not come from great wealth, but I have never heard her speak an unkind word, nor have I heard or seen her dishonor herself or her family in any way."

"A woman of honor." Father's expression softened. "And grandchildren. Yes." He drained his wine glass. "I suppose I might be able to convince your mother that the world as she knows it has not ended in light of this development. I don't envy Frank Estes, though. His wife will not be pleased."

"We already broke the news to him, Father," Byron said. "I won't lie. He is very upset, not only with me but also with you. He says he is going to force me to marry Daisy, or he'll ruin us all."

Father's eyes narrowed. "Is that what he said, did he? If he dares to challenge me, he will find he has made the biggest mistake of his life. I'll show him a thing or two about ruination. Now if this Vera girl is the one you want, you take hold of her, Byron."

Clarence chuckled. "That Gates charm wins them over every time."

"Do you boys have plans for this evening?"

"Yes, sir," Byron answered. "We'll be going out."

"Well, that's fine. Don't get in trouble."

❧

Later, the men found themselves at one of Clarence's favorite gaming haunts. Clarence motioned for Byron to join him. "Come on, old man. Let's get started."

"Uh, I think I'll sit this one out."

"What's the matter? Did Estes rob you, too?"

"You know I no longer indulge in gaming. I'll get a vicarious thrill from watching you play."

Clarence shrugged. "Whatever you say."

As Clarence played, Byron declined intoxicating beverages and studied his surroundings. Why hadn't he seen how tawdry the activities were on previous visits? Joy didn't exude from anyone, and if it did, the emotion seemed to be a poor imitation of the type of bliss Vera emanated just from the sheer delight of being alive. Why did these people suddenly seem so unlike him? Lives enslaved by Lady Luck. He shook such morose thoughts from his head. No need to take away from his friend's entertainment.

After a modest win, Clarence took a breather. "I'm ahead, old man. Are you ready to join me now? I'll even get you started." To prove his sincerity, he peeled a few bills from a wad of money he carried.

"Thanks, but no thanks."

"Really? You're not any fun to be around anymore."

"I'm a changed man. I told you so. Do you believe me now?"

"Sadly enough, I do." He sighed. "I admit I'm both disappointed and envious. But enough of that. I'm off to win more money!"

The rest of the night, Byron resisted Clarence's efforts to drag him to the tables, as well as the attempts of several women to garner his attention. He had a feeling he disappointed everyone. Everyone except himself. And the Lord.

Clarence gambled until the establishment was ready to close for the night.

"I can't believe I found you right where I left you," he remarked to Byron. "Have you even moved at all this evening?"

"Not much."

"You really are turning into an old man."

"You've called me that all your life. I might as well live up to it."

Clarence laughed. "I didn't mean it literally, old man."

"Perhaps not. So how did you do at the tables?"

Clarence lifted his palms in surrender. "I lost every penny. But I enjoyed myself. Especially since the money was all yours." Clarence laughed like a hyena, and Byron noticed that his friend's voice was slurred from drink. He watched Clarence wink at a nearby woman of plump frame, her lips and cheeks painted red.

"Come on," Byron said in Clarence's ear.

Had he looked like this in the past when he exited the gaming establishments after an evening of frolicking? And to think, he'd been afraid of this evening, afraid he'd be tempted back into his former lifestyle. Yet going to the gambling parlor with Clarence only proved to Byron that he wanted to change and to make the change a permanent one. With clarity he hadn't previously felt, he realized the evening had been a test of sorts. A test he felt he had passed.

I thank Thee, Lord!

With some effort, Byron managed to escort Clarence outside. Almost before they crossed the threshold, Clarence eyed a new man he called a "friend" and summoned him in a drunken slur. Byron tried to wave off the man, but Clarence insisted on speaking with him.

"Some other time, Clarence," Byron suggested. "If he's really your friend, he'll be available to see you another day."

"But I want to speak to him tonight."

"What's so urgent?"

"I have to know his secret. He won big, and I want to win big, too. At least when the money I'm risking is my own."

"Another time."

"No!" With the enhanced strength of a determined drunk, Clarence wrestled himself from Byron's grasp and stumbled toward the man.

"Come back!" Byron called.

"In a minute!" Clarence followed the stranger around the corner.

Worried, Byron decided to follow his friend. He hadn't taken two steps when he felt a hand clap over his mouth.

"Don't say a word, or I'll kill you." The growled threat was reinforced by a stab of what felt like the barrel of a gun in Byron's ribs. Before he could think of how to fight back, the large man shoved Byron into a waiting carriage.

fourteen

Byron's anger and indignation overcame his fear. "What is the meaning of this?" he demanded as the carriage jerked to a start.

"You know what this is about."

"I assure you I do not." Ideas flew through his mind. Had Estes set a plan into motion to kidnap him, forcing him to wed Daisy before he could leave town? The thought left just as quickly. Despite the older man's power, arranging such a scheme would consume more than a few hours. Not only that, but Estes would never have him taken by force to be a pawn in a hasty wedding. Appearances were much too important to him. Daisy's wedding would be planned for months, a show to be covered in the *Baltimore Sun*.

Then who?

Byron thought about other enemies he might have made. Was this the work of a jealous beau? If so, Byron wanted to be sure to bring the man who held him in his grip up-to-date. The only woman he had eyes for was Vera, and from all accounts, she had no other beau. Or did she? The thought filled him with envious ire.

They stopped, and the man blindfolded Byron. He could smell the stench of the cloth, a combination of sweat and dirt. He tried not to gag. With rough ceremony, he was escorted into a building and thrown onto a wooden chair. No one spoke until Byron summoned the courage to break the silence.

"If you would kindly remove this blindfold, I would be grateful."

Rude guffaws greeted his request. "What, so you can see us? You must think we're stupid."

Byron debated whether or not to point out that his loss of vision enabled him to observe their voices more closely. He could easily identify them thanks to one's thick Boston accent and the other's scratchy timbre, surely the result of too many years spent in the clogged city air. He decided not to press his luck, opting instead to concentrate on something other than the smell of the cloth covering his eyes.

"You deserve no consideration," the Bostonian growled.

"Listen, if you or the man you're working for, believe I stole his sweetheart—"

The man let out an ugly laugh. "A ladies' man, eh? No, I am not a man led by jealousy. If I was, you'd be dead by now."

Dead. Byron tried not to show his fear by a nervous twitch or swallowing.

His captor continued. "And if you don't do as I say, you may well end up in a ditch. I have no mercy on deadbeats."

The term came as a shock. "Deadbeats? Why, I owe no one any money."

He felt a fist hit his gut. A loud grunt of pain left his lips. Now that they were playing roughly, he steeled himself for blows he couldn't predict. He had to weigh his words carefully to keep from angering them further.

"You owe me money. Lots of it," said Scratchy Throat. "And you are going to pay me or else."

"I would be glad to pay you, if I knew who you were."

"You don't know me by sight, and you never will. I work for the owner of the establishment you tried to rob, and though his card dealers might be softhearted, you will not find me so."

In his mind, Byron ticked off each gaming hall he had entered in the past two years. Recalling no unresolved debt, he stalled. "I admit I was a gambler, but no more."

The fist made contact a second time. The pain left Byron out of breath.

"That's what I think of liars! You wouldn't have been in a gaming hall tonight if you weren't a gambler."

Byron resisted the impulse to explain all. Yet to bring Clarence into the situation would only put his friend in danger, as well. He could only hope that Clarence wasn't experiencing similar terror elsewhere. "You run a fine hall indeed."

"It's not my gaming hall!" The fist hit him a third time. "And if you think it is, then you'll be getting more of the same, only worse. I have spies everywhere, I can track your every move if I choose."

Byron didn't believe the man on the first claim, but he had a feeling he could follow up on the second. He remained silent.

"Now see here. You owe my employer the sum total of one thousand dollars, and I intend to collect. You are to meet me in front of Jay's Haberdashery in one fortnight to the hour with the money."

"And if I refuse?" Byron hardened his abdominal muscles and took the blow that followed.

"You like a fist in yer belly? Then you'll be gettin' more of the same."

"The police have a hard bed and a diet of bread and water for extortionists," Byron spat.

"If you call the police or try to get out of your obligation, Miss Daisy Estes will be the one sitting in this chair the next time."

He froze. "You wouldn't dare."

"Oh, wouldn't I? I have no respect for women who keep company with men like you." The man paused. "Now do you understand, or do you need another blow to the gut?"

His abdomen throbbing, Byron fought the urge to wince. "No. No. I understand. I'll get the money."

"See to it that you do."

They took Byron back to the carriage, where everyone remained silent. Byron's thoughts went back and forth between deciding how to procure such a sum quickly and figuring out how he would conceal his plight from his parents, who had cautioned him against gaming. And of course he wanted to keep Clarence out of the whole mess—and Vera. What would she think if she could see him now, helpless and threatened? He shuddered.

The vehicle stopped. They removed the blindfold and threw Byron on the street in front of the gaming hall where they had plucked him. He would have landed on his knees had he not caught himself in time, landing on both feet with athletic agility.

Stunned, he rubbed his gut where he had been battered, but he managed to rise to his feet. He brushed off his clothes, righted his stance, and went inside the gaming hall. Surely Clarence had gone back in once he saw that Byron had disappeared.

He was thankful to discover that he was right; his friend awaited. He wished Clarence hadn't used the extra time to consume another drink or two, making his posture slack. However, he wasn't about to complain.

"Where were you, old boy?" Clarence asked, his voice even more slurred. "I looked around and couldn't find you."

"I thank you for not leaving me stranded in this part of town without transportation," Byron noted. "But as for explanations, you'll have to wait until later. When you're sober."

"But I wanna know now!" Clarence hiccupped.

Byron hissed in his ear, "Don't make a scene. I'll explain all later."

"You bet your life you will."

Byron didn't even want to joke about the truth given Clarence's drunken state.

The next half hour was spent getting Clarence home and up to his guest chamber without Byron's parents seeing. Though he and Clarence were grown men, Byron didn't like the idea of bringing an inebriated friend into his parents' home, but the situation couldn't be avoided. He said a silent prayer asking forgiveness for not honoring his parents as they deserved.

Byron's faithful valet met them in the hall just as he led his wayward friend into the bedroom. "May I be of assistance, sir?"

"Yes, Philemon. Please undress him. I can take care of myself this evening."

"Very good, sir. I have already laid your nightclothes on your bed."

"Very good. And will you get Mr. Stanley some coffee? Make it strong."

"The spoon will stand up in the cup, sir."

Seeing his clothes awaiting him on the overstuffed mattress reminded Byron just how tired he was. His hours had become earlier on both ends of the day during his stay in the country, and he was no longer accustomed to staying out late. The fact that he only ran into trouble in the dead of night didn't escape his notice. Was God trying to tell him something? For the moment he brushed aside the idea.

Byron hadn't begun undressing when the valet stepped back in. "Mr. Stanley is asking for you, sir."

Byron yawned. "Tell him I'll talk to him tomorrow."

"Due to the late hour, I made that suggestion, but I'm afraid he's quite insistent. He says he won't sleep until he's seen you. I tried to quiet him, but the more I tried to speak to him logically—but with utmost respect, I assure you—the louder his voice became. I know you don't wish to awaken your parents, sir."

Byron sighed. "Right you are. Tell him I will see him."

"Yes. So sorry I could not be of more assistance, sir."

"That is quite all right. I know how Clarence gets when he's, shall we say, under the weather."

Philemon chuckled. "Yes, sir."

Byron opted to stay in his evening clothes long enough to see Clarence. He stepped into the next room.

Clarence was lying on the bed. He seemed small in the oversized guest bed with its heavy canopy and thick blue coverlet.

"Are you asleep?"

Clarence groaned.

"We can talk tomorrow," Byron suggested.

"No. No. I want to know what happened." His bloodshot eyes narrowed, and he studied Byron with a crooked neck. "Is it me, or do you seem a little bit cagey? You know, I'm used to hiding things, so I can tell when a man's not forthcoming with the truth. Don't deny that something happened. So tell me, what was it?" Clarence burped and looked at the canopy. "If only I could stop the bed from spinning. . ."

Byron shook his head, glad that he hadn't partaken of strong drink. "Are you sure you want to talk tonight?"

"Yes."

"All right, then. While you were socializing with your new friend, I was kidnapped."

"Kidnapped?" Still in a horizontal position, Clarence turned his head to look at Byron. "Where was I?"

"Making a new friend."

"Oh." A chagrined look covered Clarence's face before he recovered. "Then you must be drunker than I am, old man. If you were kidnapped, you wouldn't be standing here. Unless you're an apparition."

Byron knew better than to believe Clarence thought he was a ghost even in his most intoxicated condition. He tried not to allow irritation to slip into his voice. "I was kidnapped but, obviously, returned to the gaming hall."

"Oh. Someone wanted to talk to you, then." His eyes sharpened. "Who? A jealous lover, no doubt."

Byron leaned against the bedpost. "A jealous lover I could handle, especially since I am seeing no one but Vera at present, and I am sure she has no other suitor waiting in the wings. No, this was much more serious. And much more mysterious. The men who talked to me said I owe them money. Lots of it."

"Oh. That's strange. Who were they?"

"If only I could tell you, but I was blindfolded."

"Blindfolded?"

"Yes. They let on that they are men hired to collect debts. I think I could recognize them by voice."

"I wouldn't try to memorize their voices too closely if I were you," Clarence advised. "You have the means. Just pay off the debt you owe and forget them. Forget you ever heard them."

"Good advice. Advice I would take if only I did owe money."

Clarence rubbed his temple. "You don't? Doesn't every gambling man owe someone?"

"I gambled in the past but not anymore. And you know how meticulous I am about paying my debts to everyone from the ragman to the gaming halls. Especially the gaming halls, because they have no compunction about playing nasty games with people who owe them money. Like the one they played with me tonight."

Clarence managed to lift his shoulders up and back, even though he remained in bed. His nightshirt rubbed against the sheets, making a scratching sound. "Like I said, you'd better pay and forget it."

"No. A true debt, I'll pay. But not something trumped up. One must never give in to the demands of an extortionist, Clarence. A man such as that is never satisfied. He'll ask for more and more money until there is no more. If I agree to his terms, I'll die a broken man."

Clarence managed a shrug despite his prone position. "Then don't pay. It's your life."

"If only my life were the sole consideration. What disturbs me is that they threatened Daisy."

"Daisy? What does she have to do with your gambling debts, real or fictional?"

"Nothing, except that I have a past connection with her—"

"A very, very recent past connection," Clarence reminded him.

"Yes. And their willingness to threaten her means they know me."

"Or at least know quite a bit about you."

"Yes." Byron paused. "So what can you do to enlighten me?"

"What makes you think I know anything?"

"You're a gambler, well-known at the local gaming parlors. They said they worked for the owner of the gaming parlor, but I don't believe it. I think they are opportunists or worse," Byron told him. "I was hoping you might have learned about any local thugs causing trouble."

"You're the one who lives here, old man. Funny you should think I know more than you do. Nevertheless, I do not. And if I did, I'd certainly help you." Clarence placed his hand on his forehead. "But I have a feeling that my head will be throbbing too much tomorrow for me to be of much help to anyone."

"Perhaps, but can you remember gossip tonight? You are saying you've heard nothing about a gang of kidnapping thieves?"

Clarence shook his head.

"And you saw nothing this evening that could help us identify the men who took me?"

"No."

Byron's raised pitch showed his desperation. "No carriage? No figures in the shadows? Nothing?"

Clarence shook his head no each time. He groaned. "Uh, I'm not feeling so well. I think you'd better go."

fifteen

Moments later, Byron shut the door of his own room behind him. Exhausted, he wanted nothing more than to ask the valet for assistance in dressing but resisted the urge, knowing that Clarence was in worse condition than he and therefore was in greater need of Philemon's assistance.

Undressing, Byron sighed. Though he and Daisy were no longer connected, she was mired in his past mistakes. The past. If only he could erase it, go back, and live a more Christian life. But he couldn't. Though the Lord had saved him from eternal damnation, Byron would have to face the consequences of the poor choices he had made. The time to face them was now.

Would the men really harm Daisy if he didn't pay the money? The thought sent a chill through his back.

Maybe Clarence was right. Maybe he should just pay the money and consider it a gambling loss. But at the same time, to pay criminals would not be rightful retribution for past wrongs; he would simply be buying off dishonest men. He couldn't bring himself to be at peace with such a notion.

Heavenly Father, Thou hast heard more from me these past few weeks than Thou hast heard over the rest of my lifetime. Still, I beseech Thee to forgive me for my past and to protect Daisy and any other person—Byron swallowed—*especially Vera—who may be affected today by my past mistakes. I pray for knowledge regarding my next course of action and the courage to carry forth Thy answer, whatever that might be. I ask Thee, since I am of weak spirit and flesh, to be clear in Thy communication with me, lest I falter so soon on my new journey with Thee. In the name of Thy Son Jesus, amen.*

As Byron slipped into bed, he could think only of one person. Vera. He expected a flush of romantic feelings and yearnings to accompany her presence in his mind, but to his surprise, they did not. Instead, he felt a more benevolent emotion, one that seemed to say that Vera could somehow offer him help and protection. But how? He knew without a doubt that Vera had never stepped foot within a hundred yards of any gaming hall. Had he still been a betting man, he would have wagered his very life on that premise. So why did he feel the urge to confide in Vera?

Without warning, the answer presented itself. She was praying for him.

He had to come out of this situation a better man, a man more worthy of the one he loved. This was a test, a difficult one.

He prayed he wouldn't fail.

৯

Alone in her bedroom, Vera tried to concentrate on the blanket she crocheted in anticipation of Alice's new baby. She wanted to keep the gift a secret until after the birth, so she had made a habit of retiring early and stitching a row or two before nightly devotions. Not knowing whether the new arrival would be a boy or girl, Vera had selected a soft white yarn.

She let out a moan when she realized the last few stitches were too tight. Did they betray how tense she felt? Pulling them out, she decided nervousness had shown itself all day. A vase had nearly met its doom earlier as she nipped it with the feather duster, and a batch of rolls had to make an appearance at the dinner table too brown on the edges and top.

Lord, please console me. You know I will not rest until Byron returns safely. I pray that my constant petitions on his behalf have kept him safe. Bring him back to me soon and in one piece, I beg of Thee. In Jesus' name, amen.

❧

The next day, Byron's train headed west into rural Maryland. He had parted Baltimore amid his mother's remonstrances that he should return soon. Clarence had been quiet at breakfast, but if Byron's parents noticed his unusual condition, they refrained from commenting. Clarence rubbed his temple and groaned. "I wish I had stopped before I put down that last pint of ale."

"You say that today, but will you feel the same way the next time someone offers you libations?"

"I can't answer that, old man." Clarence sighed and leaned back in his seat. "I wish I could be more like you in being good."

"More like me? I never thought I'd hear you say that. At least, not now that I have changed."

Clarence's grin was wry. "I didn't either. But I do admire your strength and fortitude in keeping your resolution."

Byron studied his friend. "Why do I have a feeling there's something more?"

"You really do want to shame me, don't you?" As Byron shook his head, Clarence continued, "I know I made fun of Vera in the past, but I can see by the way you look at each other and how you can seem to think of nothing but her health and happiness that the two of you have grown to love each other."

"My feelings toward Vera are quite different than past flirtations. I find them much more rewarding. I hope she does, as well," Byron offered.

"I think she does. I admit I used to envy you and the number of comely women you attracted, but now that I witness you involved in something deeper, I must say your position is more enviable now," Clarence admitted. "You are on your way to seeing a woman who truly loves you. But I? I have only gambling losses and no woman to grow fond of me for more than a brief interlude of games of chance."

"Might I suggest that you school yourself in a lesson I had to learn for myself? If you regarded your dealings with women as more than sport, the women might return your affections."

"That is a thought I'm willing to consider."

"I have a feeling my kidnapping has something to do with your contemplations."

Clarence regarded Byron through bloodshot eyes. "You would be right."

Byron wanted to remind Clarence that the Lord was the true reason for the positive changes, but as Clarence sat back and shut his eyes in repose, Byron decided the time wasn't right. Other opportunities would present themselves.

Instead, he looked at passing scenery and concentrated on Vera. Images of her entered his mind. Welcome portraits of her flawless face framed by lovely blond locks danced as lively as her eyes.

Not bothering to stop for dinner, as soon as he arrived at Clarence's, Byron jumped right on his horse and rode to the Sharpe farm. As he passed through the leafy Maryland countryside, his troubles melted away. All he could think of was his beloved Vera.

Finally, he arrived and then knocked on the back door of the Sharpes' farmhouse. Vera answered.

"Byron! You're home already?" Her face looked even more beautiful than he remembered. Her complexion seemed creamier despite harsh sunlight, her image more ethereal than she had appeared in his wildest imaginings while he was in Baltimore. Perhaps her heightened appearance resulted from a glow of happiness.

"Yes." His voice caught. "I missed you so."

"And I, you."

Unable to resist the urge, he took her hands in his and gave them a light squeeze. She looked down at their hands gripping one another and returned the gesture. How was it that a woman's hands could feel so soft yet exude such gentle strength?

To his regret, she let go of his grasp. "Come in," she whispered. "Alice and the baby are asleep."

"That's right. Their afternoon nap. Alice is going to think I do this on purpose."

Vera let out a musical laugh. "I like that idea just fine. It gives us time to talk."

"Indeed it does." Despite his nonchalant response, Byron didn't remember a time when he had felt more anxiety. It occurred to him that his pride was at stake, an emotion in which he had invested an inordinate amount of time. Was God telling him it was time to let go of his pride?

"Are you hungry? I can look and see if Elmer didn't make off with the last slice of pie."

"No, thank you. I couldn't eat anything now if I tried."

"Something to drink, then?" she offered. "Tea or lemonade?"

He shook his head and noted that the temperature in the kitchen felt pleasant.

Vera glanced past him toward the nursery door. "Maybe we should go outside, lest we wake them."

"That might not be a bad idea. I was just thinking that we won't have pleasant weather much longer."

"Yes. All the more reason to enjoy warm sunshine now."

The couple crossed the back porch and headed toward the familiar wicker chairs. As soon as he sat facing Vera, Byron noticed that the sun shone in one direction; but behind Vera, a huge row of black clouds threatened rain from the southwest.

"Don't keep me waiting," Vera pleaded. "Tell me everything that happened. I want you to know first, though, that I prayed for your safe return the entire time you were gone."

Byron remembered how the gaming hall held no appeal for him that night. Surely Vera had been praying for him at that moment. "Believe me, at times I felt your prayers."

With an attitude of humility, Byron revealed to her what happened. First he told her how Daisy agreed that they shouldn't wed, and about Mr. Estes's emotional response to the news that the Gates and Estes families would not be joined together in marriage.

"Oh, I'm so sorry, Byron. How awful for you to feel you disappointed them. But surely they didn't think they could force the two of you to marry."

"They grew up in another era with different expectations, but even now in our social set, family alliances sometimes override individual consideration when it comes to marriage."

"You make it sound like dynasties based on royal bloodlines."

Byron chuckled. "Some of the people in my set fancy themselves to be royalty."

Vera didn't chuckle along with him. Her increased rate of breathing told him that he was upsetting her and making his family and friends sound intimidating. He thought about Daisy and her flippant attitude toward life and spirituality. He wished he could tell Vera that the two of them would be the best of friends. Yet he couldn't. Daisy didn't possess the depth of character to appreciate someone like Vera.

He cleared his throat. "The ones who are my real friends aren't like that at all. If I valued matching powerful families through marriage so much, don't you think I'd have married Daisy long ago?" A raindrop touched upon his shoulder.

She exhaled. "You have a point. And I must admit, I feel better knowing that Miss Estes didn't seem in the least upset. I hope that fact didn't bruise your pride too much."

"Not so much. Miss Estes will never lose her place in my heart as a cherished childhood friend." More raindrops followed.

"What a relief that's all settled. Now you can relax."

He noticed droplets wetting her hair. "If only that were so."

Her eyes widened. "There's something more?"

"Regrettably." He peered at the dark sky. "Look, Vera, do you think your sister is still sleeping?"

She nodded. "She usually doesn't awaken until at least four."

"Then let's at least go to the porch to get out of this rain. I'd hate to see you catch a cold."

"Me, too." She grimaced as more droplets hit her face. "It doesn't look like this rain will stop any time soon."

They hurried on the porch and watched the shower for a few moments. All was pleasant until a crack of lightning roared through the sky, striking a tune with a clap of thunder that seemed too close for comfort. Wind blew raindrops into their faces.

"Maybe we'd better go in," Vera suggested.

Byron nodded.

They crossed the threshold as the downpour approached from the western pasture.

sixteen

Byron knew that had Vera not been so eager to hear about his trip, she would have observed the formality of escorting him into the parlor. He took the oak chair beside hers. "I hope Mrs. Sharpe won't mind my presence in her kitchen too much."

"My sister will warm up to you once she sees that she can do without me around here and that you really have changed." Vera paused. "Alice can't help the fact that she still worries. She thinks it is terribly hard to change, and I suppose she's right."

"It is, but you can believe me when I say I have. Why, I was even able to resist gambling when I went into a gaming hall."

Her eyes widened. "I beg your pardon?"

"Remember how I told you I planned to take Clarence out for a night on the town?"

"Yes, but I suppose I thought you'd be seeing a play or having dinner at a hotel. I feel so stupid. I should have known that gambling would be involved."

"No, no. You should never feel stupid. In fact, I wish we had confined ourselves to the activities you suggest. I would have enjoyed our outing much more. But Clarence insisted on the gaming hall."

"I have no doubt you speak the truth." She swallowed. "So you—you gave in to temptation?"

"What do you mean?"

"You gambled?" she asked.

"No. No, I didn't. I only watched Clarence."

"You weren't the least bit tempted?"

He shrugged. "Maybe for an instant, but any allure the tables once held for me soon passed."

She sighed. "So my prayers were answered in the way we had hoped."

"I'm more than willing to come to that conclusion." He reached for her hands once more. She allowed him to take them in his. Their warmth consoled him. "I want to thank you, Vera."

"For my prayers?"

"Unequivocally. For the first time in my life, I could see how the people there, though seeking fun, were the most miserable lot one could ever hope to see. I do not exaggerate when I say they looked like the walking dead. At least they did in my eyes. Vera, please know that I have no desire ever to go into another gaming hall."

"Really?"

"Really. Perhaps I shouldn't have revealed to you that I went. The fact that Clarence insisted is no excuse, and I won't let him cajole me next time."

"But you admit your folly. And that shows how much you have changed from the man you were rumored to be."

"Good." Her words fortified him, and he pressed onward to assure her. "I am determined not to be anything but straightforward. I can only throw myself on your mercy and hope you will understand. I think, somewhere in my heart, that I needed to go back so God could show me the extent of my former folly." He took in a breath. "And if that weren't enough, He made sure to give me the message loudly and clearly by the next event that happened."

She clasped at her throat. "I'm not sure how much more news I can take in a day."

"I don't have to tell you, then."

"Oh, do tell me. I'd rather know than wonder."

Byron relayed his account about the kidnapping and threats. She listened intently, not interrupting. "So you see, though I am a changed man today, my association with elements from my past life have come back to haunt me."

This time, she was the one who clutched his hands as though she never wanted to let go. Byron thought this not an unpleasant development.

He studied her. "Vera, you're trembling."

"I–I'm sorry." She let go of his grip.

He wanted to take her in his arms and console her, but she made no move to come closer to him. He decided it was best to remain at bay.

She composed herself, her body stiffening with self-assurance, either feigned or real. "I am glad you have developed enough trust in me to take me into your confidence. Yet I almost wish you had not. I am afraid for your safety now, but I fear there is nothing I can do to help you. Nothing practical, in any event. I can only advise you."

"What is your advice, my dear Vera? For surely I must take it, as God has led me to you."

She nodded. "Please. Pay the debt. It will keep you out of further danger."

He felt surprised that Vera had just shared the same advice Clarence had imparted. "But these men are extortionists, and I believe their greed for money will prove insatiable. They will continue to ask for money until there is no more, and I will be left an impoverished man."

"Is that really the way extortion works?"

"I'm afraid so. And where is the justice in paying this debt that I did not incur?"

"I will keep praying."

"Please do so, my sweet Vera. You will be the first person in Washington County to know what transpires." He tried not to allow his gaze to linger upon her pink mouth lest he take a liberty to which he was not entitled. Vera, so innocent yet so wise, deserved their first kiss to take place in the most special of circumstances, not as an impromptu gesture of farewell. He sensed that similar thoughts swam in her head. He gripped her hands and brought them to his lips, allowing them to brush the back of her knuckles. Their indescribable softness made him wish he could linger, but he let go before he changed his mind.

※

After Byron departed, Vera could hardly concentrate on dinner preparations. She washed by rote the tomatoes she had picked that morning and then peeled them with little attention. Her thoughts returned again and again to Byron. The mere touch of his lips upon her hand burned in her memory, superseding anything he could have said about gaming. She could have forgiven his error but was grateful his efforts to cultivate a relationship with Christ were proving sincere.

She mulled over the details of their visit. As always when she was near Byron, time didn't matter. She lost herself in studying his face. If he had been born in another circumstance, he surely could have been a model for shaving implements or other manly products, using his exceptional appearance to inspire men everywhere. But even such a countenance and form would not have been enough for her to long for him had he not taken the journey to live a life closer to the Lord. How could she not love a man who was her dream inside and out?

Oh Lord, I pray, now that it is finally my turn for love, that Thou wilt keep Byron safe!

Alice interrupted her thoughts. "Mr. Gates always has a way of visiting when I'm napping, doesn't he?"

Vera startled. "Oh, you scared me."

"Sorry."

"So we woke you? We didn't mean to."

"I woke up for a moment, but I turned back over." Alice rubbed her expanding belly. "What did he say?"

"He told me how he resisted temptation."

"I'm glad to hear that. How?" Alice retrieved an extra knife from the drawer and helped Vera with the peeling chore.

Vera debated about how much to tell Alice. "He realized the folly of gambling when he took Clarence, at his insistence, into a gaming hall. He told me the people there were like the walking dead."

Alice shook her head and blinked her eyes. "Byron can pack more action in one day than I can muster in a month of Sundays."

Vera laughed, enjoying the emotional outlet.

In contrast, Alice looked worried. "And you forgave him for going into such a place?"

"Of course. I am not his judge."

"I would never forgive Elmer if he did any such thing," Alice said.

"Elmer is not Byron. Your husband has never been tempted to gamble and has no need to overcome the urge by facing— and defeating—his temptation."

Alice clucked. "You have set your heart afire for Byron Gates. I hope it doesn't burn to the point of destruction."

"It only burns with happy emotion. You may not see the circumstances as I do, but I appreciate his willingness to be honest. Most men would have never confided such detail."

"True."

Vera relished the victory of Alice's approval and then ventured a query. "Alice?"

"Yes?"

Vera swallowed. "Would you pray for Byron?"

Alice stopped slicing her tomato. "I know the scriptures. You're just trying to get me to soften my heart to him, aren't you?"

Vera chuckled. "I wouldn't mind that. But he could use our prayers. Please believe me when I tell you this."

Alice sent her a reluctant sigh. "Oh, all right. I'll pray for him."

"Thank you."

"But still, why do I think there's something you're not telling me?"

"He did confide in me, and his willingness to be so forthright with me proved to me that our relationship is grounded in trust and is honest."

"He confided in you? How unusual it is for a man to confide anything important to a woman," Alice noted. "What, pray tell, is this confidence?"

"I cannot reveal it to you or anyone else. That is why it is called a confidence," Vera said quietly. "Perhaps you have misjudged Byron, Alice. Perhaps all of us did."

"For your sake, I hope I have."

Vera didn't answer. How could she tell her sister that Byron's admission only made her love him more?

"You've fallen in love with him, haven't you?" Alice's question sounded more like a statement.

"I—I have. And I think he may feel the same way about me."

"I was afraid he'd take you away from me. If you do marry, I shall miss you terribly. For your helping hands, certainly, but for your company, too. There's a reason why you were paid to be a companion to Mrs. Alden, you know."

Vera twisted her mouth into a wry grin. "I think my ability to listen helped me more than my attempts at conversation."

"You are well read and keep up with the times. I'm sure she enjoyed talking to you very much," Alice said. "I know she must miss you, judging from the frequency of her correspondence to you. And even though Elmer would hire a nurse and a maid to help me should you leave, no other person in your capacity could ever give little Paul the love that you do."

"True. But I would never move so far away that I couldn't see you often. I would never, ever leave my Maryland."

seventeen

After a fortnight had passed and at the appointed wee hour, Byron stood on the poorly lighted corner in front of Jay's Haberdashery. The store's pretentious name befitted its location in the business district. But to its left was a pitch-black street that led to Baltimore's northern docks.

Byron's palms sweated as he waited to meet his kidnappers. He hadn't summoned the police, a fact he regretted. Cover of night would hide the identities of the criminals, but Byron was determined to observe as much as possible about them.

Lord, put Thy hand upon me, and grant me Thy protection.

Byron also remembered that someone more worthy than he was praying for him right at that moment as they had agreed. Surely the Lord would listen to the plea of Vera Howard.

From the dark street behind him, Bostonian's voice interrupted his pleading. "Good. You showed up. Smart fellow. You better not have any police waitin' for us. If you do, you'll be sorry."

Scratchy Throat whispered, "Step back to us, and don't be turnin' around."

Byron could tell that the man meant what he said. They had both seemed large the night they kidnapped him; tonight they sounded even larger. He swallowed and complied. "I still maintain that I am a man of honor, in my way, and I don't owe anyone this sum of money. But for the sake of Miss Estes—"

"We don't got time for speechifyin'. We just want our money," said Scratchy Throat.

Unaccustomed to being interrupted in midsentence, Byron bit back the urge to reprimand the criminal for his rudeness. Instead, he handed over the sack of bills.

The Bostonian grabbed the loot and then tilted his head toward his companion. "You watch him while I count. I don't take kindly to any man who tries to rob us."

Byron wanted to blurt that he, not Byron, was the robber, but decided his life could depend on his ability to hold his tongue.

As the Bostonian leaned forward into the edge of light so he could see the bills, Scratchy Throat kept what felt like a gun barrel against Byron's ribs.

Please, Lord, I have learned my lesson. I never want to return to my past ways. And I never will. Let them just take their money so this can be the end of this ordeal and I can get on with the rest of my life.

The Bostonian looked up and growled. "What's the meaning of this?"

"I beg your pardon?" Byron said.

"It's not all here."

"Surely you're mistaken," Byron responded with a stammer. He felt the gun barrel poke more deeply into his side. "I watched the bank clerk count out the bills myself. Then I counted the money again just before I left my room. I'm not holding back any of it. It's all there. I promise."

"It's only one thousand dollars."

Genuine confusion visited Byron. "Only? But that was the amount we agreed upon."

"No, we need fifteen hundred."

Byron tried to swallow but couldn't. His worst fears had materialized. These evil men were not out to collect an honest, if mistaken, debt. They truly were extortionists, planning to keep him dangling with their threat to harm Daisy if he didn't give them more money. How long would they keep him mired in their scheme? Where would it end? How much money would it take to satisfy them? And how would he be able to obtain additional funds? He didn't like the feeling of desperation such musings brought to his mind.

He decided to appeal to whatever humanity the criminals might possess. "See here now, I apparently misunderstood. It was an honest mistake."

Scratchy Throat snorted. "He says his so-called mistake was honest. Like we think he's an honest man. Ha."

Byron ignored the insult. "Look here, you made one thousand dollars with a small amount of effort and no resistance on my part. Why can't we all be gentlemen here and call our business an even exchange?"

"But you owe us a third again of what you gave us," the Bostonian said. "I think that is too much for our boss to overlook."

Byron resisted the urge to point out that the alleged debt was half again what he had already given them, not a third.

"Yeah," said his companion. The gun dug deeper.

Byron saw no other alternative than to agree. "All right, then. I'll get you the extra money. When shall we meet?"

"Tomorrow."

"Tomorrow?" Byron shuddered. "I'm sorry, but even under the most ideal circumstances, I cannot come up with that kind of money so soon. I need at least a week."

"I don't think so. Tomorrow."

"Father in heaven, I've been such a fool." Byron hadn't meant to utter the words, but they flew into the night air with intensity.

The Bostonian guffawed. "What's that, you say? A prayer? What makes a gambling man like you think he can get the

Man Upstairs to answer his plea?"

"I'll bet you this here gambler's gettin' religion," Scratchy Throat said. "Whaddya say, boss? Ya wanna take that bet?" An ugly laugh filled the air.

The Bostonian shushed him. "Do you want to call attention to us, you fool?"

A well-dressed man crossed the lighted thoroughfare at that moment. "See now, gentlemen, is there some kind of trouble here?"

Byron looked into the man's face, which shone clearly from his approaching position relative to the streetlight in front of the haberdashery. Afraid for his would-be rescuer, Byron sent the man a slight shake of his head to warn that trouble could ensue, and he braced himself to feel the tip of the weapon jab his rib. But the renewed threat never occurred.

"Is there some way I may be of assistance, Mr. Ames?" The fair-haired man addressed the Bostonian and stepped onto the corner, with Byron on his left.

"How did you know—" He took in a breath and started over. "I mean, I–I'm not Ames. You don't know me." For the first time since Byron encountered him, the Bostonian trembled. His speech became more rushed and his accent more pronounced. "And we are simply concluding a very successful meeting. I was just telling this gentleman—who we're doing business with—that I look forward to sharing a pint of ale with him next week. Isn't that right?"

He looked at Byron. At last Byron could discern the Bostonian's features. He was older than Byron had imagined, with bushy gray eyebrows and an irregularly shaped dark mole on his left cheek.

Byron repeated, "We'll be meeting here again. . .in one week's time."

"This man here doesn't need to know the boring details." The Bostonian's voice revealed more than a hint of danger.

"Right you are. By your leave, I'll be on my way. Good night, Mr. Gates." The blond set his blue-eyed stare upon Byron's waiting horse, a sure sign that Byron should make a quick exit.

"Good night." Byron took advantage of his chance to flee before the terms of the forced agreement could change. He broke away from the men and, with a practiced swagger, approached his horse, mounted, and trotted into the night.

He looked back just long enough to be sure the two criminals hadn't decided to chase him. To his relief, they had not. The men stood by the streetlight. From a distance, they looked liked statues. The blond man was nowhere to be seen.

Byron wondered how that could be, but had no inclination to contemplate the puzzle. He only wanted to escape.

After Byron had traversed a few blocks uphill toward his house, he relaxed his muscles just a bit. He allowed his horse to slow his gait, and he realized his breathing had grown ragged. Clutching at his throat, he noticed it still felt constricted. He loosened his shirt collar.

Determined to concentrate on something—anything—other than what had just happened, he tried to take notice of his surroundings. The closer he drew to his home, the more the character of the streets and houses improved. Seeing the houses of childhood playmates and friends left him feeling more secure.

Since the probability of being spotted by someone of his acquaintance was probable in spite of the lateness of the hour, Byron tried to appear casual. He said a silent prayer that his presence would not be noticed, possibly bringing up questions that could embarrass his family. Realizing how selfish he would be to leave the prayer with just a petition, he added a praise for the stranger who had saved him from trouble. Afterward, he contemplated what had transpired. Had the appearance of the stranger been an answer to prayer?

eighteen

After he had encountered the criminals, Byron couldn't get on the train heading back to the country fast enough. Despite his mother's protests at breakfast that he needed to stay in the city longer, Byron wanted to return to Vera. As they had agreed on their last meeting, he traveled by the noon train to Hagerstown and made his way directly to the Sharpe family's farm.

As soon as he saw Vera, he felt as though he had come home. Vera normally greeted him in a plain housedress, but on that day she wore her flattering green Sunday dress. The scent of rosewater emanated from her, making him want to draw nearer.

To his relief, she hurried him into the semiprivate parlor.

"What happened?" Vera wanted to know. "Oh, I was so worried about you. I've been praying my heart out."

"Thank you." He remembered the fair-haired man who had appeared just at the right time. "I have no doubt you have."

"So you made the payment, then? I was right, and you'll never see those men again?" Vera shook her head up and down rapidly, reminding Byron of a little girl trying to get her parents to agree to buy her a new doll. He smiled.

Unfortunately for Byron, Vera misinterpreted his gesture, which only made things worse. "Oh, I'm so glad!"

Byron turned his expression serious. "No, Vera. It's not like that, I'm sorry to say. The problem is still not solved. They want more money, and I'm supposed to meet them again next week."

"More money? How can that be?" A stricken look crossed her features. "You have just started being honest with me, Byron. There isn't some secret they are agreeing to keep in return for payoff, is there?"

"No. It's not blackmail but extortion. They are still threatening to hurt Daisy. And while we are not a couple, she is a friend, and I don't want to see her get hurt."

"Of course not!"

"Who's getting hurt?" Alice's voice interrupted. Holding the baby, she stood in the doorway. Her mouth had pressed itself into a fine line.

When both Byron and Vera hesitated, Alice looked at the clock. "Dinner will be ready in an hour. I suggest you stay, Mr. Gates."

"Stay for dinner?" Vera asked.

"Why, of course." Byron looked surprised but hastened to agree. He looked at Vera, hoping to see an expression of encouragement on her face. Why did she seem worried?

&

After a meal of fried chicken, mashed potatoes, and vegetables, Alice brought up the subject Vera feared most: what had really happened in Baltimore.

"You must be losing track of what is told to you, my dear," Elmer jested. "Byron has already given us an account of his trip."

"He has, has he? Not all of it. Vera herself told me he confided something important to her, and as her sister and guardian, I intend to find out what it is."

"Byron owes you no explanation," Vera objected.

"I disagree," Byron said.

"You what?" Vera asked.

"I'm sorry, Vera, but your sister is right. True, I took you into my confidence, and I'm glad I did. Once again, you have demonstrated a tremendous ability to forgive. In my view, that capacity should be emulated by all Christians."

"That doesn't mean you must tell all," Vera pointed out.

"I think it does. That is, if I am to remain a part of your life. And I do hope that will happen. I've kept secrets long enough. As the Bible says, 'The truth shall make you free.' " Without further ado, Byron explained to Alice and Elmer how he had been kidnapped and was being extorted.

"None of this is Byron's fault," Vera hastened to defend him as her sister and brother-in-law paused to digest the information. "He is a changed man."

"A changed man with a past that is still unresolved." Elmer's tone betrayed disappointment and distress rather than rage. He stared at his empty dinner plate.

"I wish I could go back and make things right," Byron told them. "I wish I could change the man I once was. Admittedly, I am facing the consequences of my past. I deserve such. But though this experience is frightening and painful, I believe I am learning more about why a life that glorifies God is better spent than one wasted in idle pursuits. Of course I would be more comfortable if my past actions didn't affect my present life, but then, what would I learn?"

"Your degree of insight is commendable," Elmer noted.

Alice crossed her arms and stared Byron in the eyes. "I'm glad you have learned your lesson, but I am reluctant to say that your confession entitles you to keep company with our Vera. She did not help you create this mess, Mr. Gates, and our good family name need not be sullied by any rumor that Vera is socializing with a betrothed man. Not when there are plenty of godly men your age right here in this community who would eagerly court her."

Vera pursed her lips. She hadn't encouraged any man. At least, not until Byron's visit. True, she had been busy tending to Alice and her new son. Even if Vera hadn't been so occupied, her reputation as a wallflower attracted no suitors. Vera was unsure of what her sister hoped to gain by attacking Byron's character.

"Luckily for me, none of those many men made their intentions known," Byron interjected.

Vera sent him a grateful look.

"So you are saying you would like to court Vera in earnest?" Elmer asked.

Byron, obviously emboldened by the suddenness of the query, blurted out, "Yes. As a matter of fact, I would. With Vera's consent, of course." He smiled at Vera.

A joyous bolt of lightning made her body quicken. "Y–yes."

"Elmer!" Alice pleaded.

Elmer shook his head at Alice and then directed his attention to Byron. "If only you had asked me in private. While I might have been open to the suggestion before today, this new development of the events in Baltimore darkens my view. You have too many loose ends—dangerous loose ends—hanging there to be free with your affections here."

"Byron will straighten out everything," Vera assured. "I know it."

"That is all well and good, and I wish you all the best," Elmer told Byron. "But until you can rise out of the mire, I cannot agree for you to pursue a courtship with my sister-in-law."

"Thank you," Alice breathed a sigh.

"Wait! Don't I have anything to say about this?" Vera asked.

"Since our parents are with the Lord in heaven, you know the answer to that. My husband is your closest male relative, and so you are to take his advice," Alice proclaimed. "I have full faith and confidence that he is saying exactly what Father would have said had he been here for you."

"Alice is right," Elmer concurred. "I am doing my best to guide you as I believe Mr. Howard would have if he were here."

"I appreciate and respect that, but—"

"No buts," Elmer said. "Byron, you can see the disruption you have caused this family. I don't believe that was your intent, but that has been the result of your involvement with Vera. I hope you will respect my wishes regarding your relationship with her."

Byron's dessert remained untouched, but he laid his napkin over it and rose from his seat. Though distress showed itself on his face, he kept his tone civil. "I understand, and I believe this should mark the conclusion of our dinner." He nodded to Alice. "Mrs. Sharpe, thank you for a lovely dinner. Mr. Sharpe, I bid you a good evening."

Before Byron could say his farewell to her, Vera spoke. "I'll see you to the door, Byron."

"That won't be necessary," Alice said.

Disgusted by Alice's constant meddling, Vera rose from her seat. "He is my guest, and I will see him to the door."

Vera rarely disobeyed a direct order from her sister, and Alice was too stunned to object. Vera noticed that Elmer tightened his lips into a thin line and shook his head ever so slightly at his wife. Though he had given in to Alice, he hadn't deserted Vera. At least he was willing to give her a moment to tell Byron good-bye.

Once they reached the front door, Vera peered back, hoping her sister wouldn't try to overhear them. She had a feeling Elmer was doing all he could to restrain his wife.

But she quickly returned her attention to Byron. She looked

into his eyes. If only he didn't have to leave.

"Are you going back to Baltimore forever?" Vera tried not to let emotion color her voice.

"I haven't decided. I must confess that your brother-in-law has given me much to contemplate. I do need to straighten out the mess in the city before I can even begin to think of courting you. Perhaps then I can be on better terms with your sister. Her approval is important to me, because I know she loves you."

"And I love her, but she can be judgmental at times."

Byron sent her a wry smile. "Yet what she said about my past affecting my present is all too true. I am not worthy of you at this time."

Eager to stop his departure, Vera touched his forearm. "I said it before, and I'll say it again. I don't care about your past sins. If God can forgive you, so can I."

"So you will see me once I release myself from the Estes family's expectations and from the extortionists?"

Vera nodded. "I shall keep you in my thoughts and prayers until the hour you return."

Byron clasped her hands and gave them a gentle squeeze. "Your prayers shall give me the strength I will need to face tomorrow."

nineteen

Since Daisy was still in Rhode Island when he returned to Baltimore, Byron prepared himself to meet with Mr. Estes alone. The butler greeted him at the door and escorted him to Mr. Estes's library.

"Well," Mr. Estes noted from his position in an overstuffed wingback chair, "here you are. I was wondering how long it would take you to come back from the country." He motioned to a waiting chair. "Sit down, sit down."

Byron obeyed.

Mr. Estes took a deep draw of his cigar. The older man blew a smoke ring and let it dissipate before looking Byron squarely in the eye. "I hope you are here to tell me that you are ready to start making serious plans with my Daisy for your upcoming nuptials."

Before meeting with the man who wanted to be his future father-in-law, Byron had contemplated how he would answer the expected query. In the past, he might have flattered Mr. Estes or even charmed his way out of the situation. Now he wanted to keep from debating while still being forthright in his communication. "I am sorry, but no. We still do not wish to marry. I don't know what else to say."

"You can simply say that you will go forward and fulfill your commitment to this family. I know you're scared, but that will wear off soon enough. Trust me."

"I don't find marriage to Daisy nearly as scary as what happened to me the other night."

"Oh?"

"It is a grave matter. I hate even to discuss it, but I feel that I should be forthright," Byron explained. "It has something to do with my past."

"Oh, that." Mr. Estes leaned over and patted Byron on the knee. "Now, now, we men all have our little skeletons in the closet—things we want to keep confidential. Not that everything about your life is a secret. But I can tell you, Mrs. Estes doesn't know every folly I committed as a bachelor. As the saying goes, boys will be boys. A few little misadventures are all part of growing up, readying you for the responsibilities of manhood. I did see your father at the club the other day, and he tells me you're just about ready to take the mantle of the business from him."

Not so long ago, that idea had struck fear into Byron's heart. But when Mr. Estes introduced the prospect at the moment, a surge of awe filled him instead.

Mr. Estes continued, "His willingness to retire and leave his life's work in your hands tells me you are ready to take on the duties and burdens of manhood."

"I do believe I am, Mr. Estes."

"Good. Then I expect you to leave your childish things behind, as the Good Book says. And when you do, I may decide to retire myself." He paused. "You do realize what that means for you as Daisy's husband, don't you?"

"I—I'm not sure."

"That means you can combine my business with yours. The result would be a formidable enterprise. Unbeatable, really."

"Why am I not surprised by your idea," Byron mused. "Yes, that would be quite a legacy." Yet to him, the prospect of such a life didn't seem as valuable as it did to Mr. Estes.

"You are a lucky man, Byron Gates. My daughter will make

an excellent society matron, and you two will be a powerful couple here in Baltimore."

"True." The prospect of such a bright future should have been balm to Byron's ears. Yet pursuing it would mean giving up Vera. He wasn't prepared to take that step.

Daisy's father sat back and savored his cigar. "Now about that wedding date. . ."

"Thank you, but I doubt if we should discuss that yet."

"I'm getting impatient, my boy." As if to illustrate, Mr. Estes drummed his fingertips against the arm of his chair.

Byron braced himself. What he was about to say would change his life forever. "I know, but I have something too important not to tell you. You see, I was kidnapped, and money has been extorted from me, even though I was innocent and did not owe the debt the kidnappers claimed."

He stopped drumming. "What?"

Byron elaborated.

Mr. Estes listened to the story but didn't respond right away. Instead, he looked at Byron as if seeing him for the first time, taking methodical puffs of his cigar all along.

"There are so many things I wish I could change, but I can't go back," Byron noted to break the tension. "I hope you can forgive me."

"Forgiveness is not the issue. I am not your confessor." The elder man tapped his cigar and let the ashes fall in a silver tray designed for that purpose. "This is a disappointment. I knew you were loose with money, but I had no idea you had run up such outrageous debts that unsavory types would come looking for you."

"But that's just it. I didn't. I owe no gaming establishment any money. Did I gamble in the past? Yes," he admitted. "But I always paid my debts."

"Yet these people say you didn't."

"They are wrong. And they are greedy."

"Greedy, you say." Mr. Estes shook his head. "You expect me to believe that these men picked you up on the street with no rhyme or reason? I would argue that they knew you were a gambler, or else they wouldn't have chosen you."

"Yes, they did seem to know who I am. And I understand they had no way of knowing I have given up gambling."

"You say you have given it up, but I have a feeling you have no idea how difficult it can be to rid oneself of a bad habit. And this is not just any bad habit, like taking an extra dessert every night. You say you have no debts, yet these men are after you. This life you have been leading is more than just idleness. It now poses danger to your business and to your personal health, apparently." His gaze focused on Byron. "Does your father know about this?"

"No. I am hoping you will not see fit to tell him. I don't want him involved, lest the criminals believe they should go after my father's fortune as well as my own."

Mr. Estes let out a *harrumph.* "At least you are man enough not to drag everyone else down with you—for now. You know this won't end here, don't you? Before you know it, these men will bleed you—and your family coffers—dry."

"I am hoping to avoid that." Dreading the next news he had to share, Byron felt his palms sweat. "Speaking of involving others, there is something more."

"More? What else can there be?"

"I am distressed by the fact they mentioned Daisy's name."

"Mentioned her name?" In a split second, he put two and two together. "You mean, they threatened my daughter?"

"Please, do not worry. I will be paying them in full so her safety is assured."

Mr. Estes's face turned bright red, and he stubbed out his cigar. "I beg your pardon, but her safety is never assured as long as you are involved in this dilemma. A dilemma of your own making."

"I suppose you're right. I asked before, and I beg of you again—please, forgive me."

"Apologies and recriminations are not good enough. Not for me, nor for my daughter. Even Silas Jenkins, as repulsive as he is, manages to keep his nose clean."

Byron tried not to flinch. "If only I could say something that would make all of this go away. You can take my word that I am more upset by this entire situation than you could ever be."

"Is that so? Your foolishness threatened the life of my daughter. I'm willing to overlook a lot of character flaws, but this is too much!" He rose to his feet.

Byron followed suit. "What can I do to make amends?"

"I'll tell you what you can do. You can simply exit my house." Mr. Estes wagged his finger in Byron's face. "And I'll tell you one thing. If anything, anything at all happens to Daisy—if a hair on her head is touched, even a fingernail chipped—I shall hold you responsible!"

Byron realized that Mr. Estes's speech was motivated by a father's concern and anxiety. He tried to remain calm. "I understand, Mr. Estes. But I do plan to have the matter resolved by the time Daisy returns from Rhode Island. By then the culprits should be in jail, and she will be safe from harm."

"She certainly will, because I never expect you to see her again. The engagement is officially off." A sad look crossed his face. "You and Daisy would have made an excellent match, one that would have been the talk of society for ages. Your indiscretions have shattered that dream."

"I feel badly for you, sir."

"I feel even worse for whatever woman you take as a wife—if you can find such a creature."

His words made Byron all the more aware that he wasn't worthy of a fine woman such as Vera.

"Good day," Mr. Estes prodded.

"Yes, sir. But before I leave, would you do me one kind favor?"

"What is it?" Mr. Estes snapped.

"Please let Daisy know that I wish the best for her and that I pray for her happiness."

"You? Praying?" Mr. Estes scoffed. "I thought Daisy was joking the other day when she said you prayed with her."

Remorse filled Byron. "I know the idea must sound ludicrous to your ears, and I can't say I blame you. But you'll tell her, won't you?"

"All right. I will." Mr. Estes strode to the library door and opened it. "You may see your way out."

"Yes, sir. Good day."

As he exited the Estes house, Byron knew someone he wanted to inform about his progress. Without ado, he made his way to the telegraph office.

ஐ

The next day, Byron's carriage made its way to the wharves. He had taken a great risk after he visited the Estes house, a risk that he hoped would pay off in ridding him of the criminals once and for all. Ever since he had sent a courier to the police station, he had been watching his back, hoping no one unsavory had discovered the deed that defied his instructions. So far, no threats had made themselves evident. At this moment, he was on his way to meet the detective who had responded, one Jonathan Pierce.

Too nervous to think of what might happen if the extortionists found out about his correspondence with the police, Byron pondered his sudden and unexpected freedom. Living through Mr. Estes's wrath had been no picnic, but he sensed that the man who would have been his father-in-law was no longer bent on punishing him or his family. Keeping his promise to Daisy, he prayed for her and Silas.

His thoughts focused on Vera. If only his freedom meant that he could return to Washington County and claim her as his bride. But he could not. He could not offer to court any woman. None could associate with him in safety until he rid himself of the extortionists.

I know I brought this on myself, Lord. Though I do not owe this debt, had I not been at the gaming house, I doubt I would have been singled out by these men. If I had not been disobedient to Thee in the past, then I would not be suffering the consequences of my sins today. I pray that Thou wilt will keep the innocent—Daisy and Vera—from suffering along with me.

"This is it, sir," the driver announced. "Pier Five."

"Thank you." Byron disembarked and examined the spot where he and Jonathan Pierce had agreed to meet. In light of the men's threats, Byron didn't dare venture near a police station. Thankfully, the lean figure of the police detective aided by the cover of darkness on a starless night made his identity difficult to discern to the unaware. "Wait here," he instructed the driver. "This won't take long."

"Yes, sir."

Byron didn't mince words after he and the detective exchanged greetings. "So what can you tell me about the men who kidnapped me?"

"We at the department are very aware of those men. That man you know as Ames is the leader. They are a ring of extortionists who prey on men with reputations for gaming."

"The sins of my past," Byron muttered.

"What was that?"

He shook his head. "Nothing. Tell me more."

"First, can you tell me how you have responded to their demands thus far?" the detective asked.

"I've been cooperative. In fact, I plan to meet them again tonight to give them what is to be the last installment of the debt."

"The last installment, you say? You must have qualms about that since you contacted me."

"I don't want others to fall prey to their schemes, Detective. I know full well that I owe not a penny to any gaming hall, yet because they threatened the safety of the woman to whom I was engaged—"

"Was?"

"Yes. Our betrothal is no more," Byron said.

"I offer my condolences."

"Yes, the situation is regrettable. But that is neither here nor there. What concerns me now is keeping my other friends and acquaintances safe and retaining my own sense of well-being."

"And you think you can accomplish that by paying them the money they demand?"

Byron let out a breath. "I hope so."

"You are playing a dangerous game, Mr. Gates. If the way this ring of thieves has operated in the past is any indication, you will not win. As long as you continue to pay, the stakes will grow higher and higher until finally you are bankrupted. These men have already ruined two gamblers in town because their targets were too embarrassed to report them so they could be stopped. I'm glad you had the courage to come to me and tell the truth."

"I have a confession to make. I might not have been so courageous if I had still been a gambler."

The detective chuckled. "Did the men scare you into quitting?"

"No. I had sworn off gambling before then. I was only in the area to accompany a friend. The Lord has given me the strength to shed my old ways."

"The Lord, so you say?" Detective Pierce looked off into the twilight. "Too bad He wasn't there when you were being kidnapped."

Byron thought about the stranger who had intimidated the men into giving him extra time to pay. "Oh, I think He was there. He was there all along."

The detective gave him a half nod and extracted a pouch of tobacco from his vest pocket. "Will you join me in a smoke?"

"No, thank you."

He shrugged and rolled the tobacco into a crisp white paper. "I think I can help you."

"Good. What is your plan?"

The detective lit the tobacco. The resulting smoke carried with it a pungent scent tinged with sweetness. "I will accompany you to the meeting place from a distance, along with two other plainclothes detectives."

"Then what?"

"We'll watch the exchange to be sure we have enough evidence to nab them. We'll close in and apprehend them and get them off the street forever."

Byron tipped his hat in farewell. "Let's hope you're right."

twenty

Byron's hands shook ever so slightly as he got ready to make the drop of money in front of the haberdashery. Night had made its full appearance, lending a sinister element to his errand. The extortionists were already standing close to the store's corner entrance when he arrived. They stood in the shadow of the doorway, revealed partially by a streetlight.

Father in heaven, protect me!

The Bostonian advanced from the shadow and reached for the satchel as Byron tied his horse. "Hand it over."

Byron complied without debate. He surveyed the nearest alleys and flinched as his gaze covered the spot where he knew the detectives to be. They weren't visible to him, so the criminals would never suspect they were being observed. For the first time since he had appeared on the appointed corner, he felt grateful for night's cape of black.

A pleased light entered the Bostonian's eyes. "It don't look like you brought anyone, just like I said. It's good that you can follow instructions. If you hadn't, you'd be dead now."

Byron swallowed, though he remembered he was safe with the police watching.

"The money had better all be there," the criminal said.

"It is, I assure you."

He riffled through the bills and then nodded. "It looks like it's all here. That was a very wise decision on your part. Very wise."

"Good." Byron wished the detectives would make their

appearance. "This should conclude our business."

The leader closed the satchel. "Not so fast. I found out you owe us more than I was originally told."

Remembering that the extortionists were about to be captured, Byron maintained his composure, resisting the urge to protest in strong terms. "I don't understand."

"It seems you're in arrears to the tune of five thousand more dollars."

"Five thousand dollars?" A suddenly dry throat caused the words to sound like a croak.

"That's right. But since you've been so good about paying us what we demanded promptly and without incident, we're willing to show you some consideration. We are willing to accept installments of five hundred dollars a month, due the first day of each month. We'll continue to meet here unless I say otherwise."

Byron darted his gaze to the alley and back. "And if I object?"

"We'll be keeping an eye on Miss Daisy Estes."

He winced. "Miss Estes and I are no longer engaged."

"Is that so?"

Though he didn't allow himself a sigh of relief, Byron thought for the briefest of moments that he had won a victory.

The extortionist didn't allow him to celebrate long. "Well then, the rumors about your sweet girl in the country must be true."

Byron shivered. He couldn't let Vera be endangered. "You know how rumors are. It's hard to separate truth from fiction."

"You'd like that, wouldn't you? As if we couldn't find out anything we wanted to know about you." The Bostonian let the words hang in the night air. "Maybe you're tryin' to take us for fools. I promise you that won't happen. We'll make it our business to find out what woman in your life means the most to you. Maybe your mother."

"You leave my mother out of this." Byron's voice sounded so threatening that he barely recognized it as his own.

The men let out ugly laughs. Byron would have sent blows to both their faces except for what he saw. Detective Pierce and the two other men approached in silence but with haste from behind the men. The officers had drawn their pistols.

"Hold it right there. You're under arrest." Detective Pierce's voice sounded menacing.

Before either man could react, the plainclothes officers grabbed each of them. The first officer wrestled the Bostonian to the ground, locking him into position with his knees. Scratchy Throat struggled until the officer dealing with him seemed to have no choice but to shove him against the side of the haberdashery. As two more officers joined in the takedown, the criminals realized they were outnumbered, and they offered no more resistance. Detective Pierce snatched Byron's money from the Bostonian, who relinquished it with a disappointed grunt. Then, searching the extortionists, the officers confiscated two pistols.

"See here, what's the meaning of this?" the leader demanded.

Pierce didn't back down. "I repeat, you're under arrest."

"On what charges? Don't three friends have every right to greet one another on the street?" the Bostonian asked.

"You won't get out of this that easily," Detective Pierce growled. "We heard everything."

"It's not what you think. He. . .he was merely paying a bill. A debt he owed us," the criminal tried to explain. "Why, he's nothin' but a rake and a gambler. See here, officer, why don't you let us take care of our own? You have no need to deal with the likes of such a lowlife."

Byron kept his face unreadable, yet the man's words hurt. He had never denied he was once a gambler and rake, but he had no idea that even criminals looked down their noses at him. The bold statement made him realize how wise he had been to turn his life over to God—not for the sake of his reputation or the opinions of others, but for the health of his soul.

"I doubt that Mr. Gates is concerned about your opinion of him," Detective Pierce observed. "But we have plenty of people planted in every gaming hall in town, and we know that he owed no gaming establishment, including the one you said you represent, any money. According to our sources, except for the night you abducted him, Mr. Gates has not darkened the door of a gaming hall in months."

"But—"

"I'll not hear any more arguments." He nodded to the others. "Load them in the wagon, boys."

As he watched his tormenters being carted off by burly officers, Byron allowed himself a relieved sigh. "For a minute there, I was wondering if you'd show up at all."

"Oh, we never let your safety become threatened. But since the leader was so talkative, we held back until we were able to get the full case against them and prove your claim of extortion. You can rest assured that they won't be bothering you or anyone else for a long time."

Byron noticed that his palms had ceased to sweat. "Thank you."

"Be sure we have your current address," Pierce advised. "We'll be needing your testimony in court when their trial comes up."

"I'll be there."

The detective handed Byron the bag, which Byron accepted. "I'm sorry," the officer said, "but I doubt we can get the rest of the money back for you."

"The first installment?" Byron confirmed. "As much as I would like to claim that money as my own, I realize now that such a sum is a small price to pay for a valuable lesson. I hate to contemplate the fortune I wasted on such pointless amusement."

"Perhaps all amusement could be considered pointless if one takes that viewpoint."

Byron pondered the idea. "I suppose some forms of entertainment are more pointless than others. In any event, I will be spending my idle moments in activities that will prove more uplifting to both body and soul. I am grateful that God has shown me mercy by sparing me much greater consequences for my sins."

"Yes, that's commendable. Save the preaching for the choir, Mr. Gates. I'd better bid you a good night. The wagon awaits, and I've got work to do. In the meantime, the city of Baltimore thanks you for possessing the courage to help us catch these extortionists."

As Byron made his way back to his childhood home, he felt relieved and gratified until he realized that he might suffer the greatest battle of all—convincing Vera's family that he was worthy of her. A wry thought crossed his mind: He couldn't convince them because indeed he wasn't good enough, and he never would be. All he could do was to show them that he really did want to stay committed to Christ and that, with Vera's help, he would stay on the path. He had to fight for her, and he would. He couldn't lose Vera.

❧

Vera tried to concentrate on her stack of mending but to no avail. All she could think about lately was how Byron had fared in Baltimore. What man could be safe meeting with known criminals? Worry visited her too often.

She knew one fact: He had been successful in breaking his engagement with Daisy. His message contained no further news. She had been praying for the Lord's protection for Byron ever since.

Clarence sent word that Byron planned to return. The closer his scheduled return date approached, the more jittery she felt.

"My, but you seem slow today, Vera," Alice noted from the rocking chair near Vera's. "I do believe I'm several socks ahead of you in darning."

"You haven't changed since we were girls. You always did like to challenge me by how fast you could complete your chores."

"And I always won," Alice pointed out.

"Might I remind you that I have no incentive to speed now. These socks belong to your husband, not to mine," Vera teased.

"Yes, and though we don't compete with one another as we once did, I might remind you that you have grown plodding in your work lately. You don't seem to be able to concentrate on your chores." Alice sighed and shook her head at her sister. "You can't stop thinking about Byron Gates, can you?"

"No," she admitted. "He's due back from Baltimore soon, and I keep praying all will be resolved upon his return."

"Mr. Gates seems to be a determined man." Alice set the sock she was darning in her lap. "Still, I have my reservations. Nothing I can say to you will change your mind about him, will it?"

"I'm afraid not."

"I suppose there is no arguing with passion. Too bad you couldn't have fallen in love with a man as fine as my Elmer instead of a cad like Byron Gates."

"I understand you want what's best for me, and I suppose if

the situation were reversed, I would share your feelings. But Byron is no longer a cad. I just know it."

"I only hope that your idea is not just wishful thinking."

"Even you must admit that you haven't seen or heard of Byron engaging in any untoward behavior since you first met him."

Alice contemplated the idea. Her furrowed brow and pursed lips told Vera she was thinking a little too hard to find something unfavorable to say. "No, I must say I can't think of anything. I haven't heard a whisper of impropriety."

"And Elmer seems to like him well enough."

"Elmer always had a soft spot in his heart for you." Without warning, Alice sniffled and kept her eyes focused on the sock.

"Alice!" Vera exclaimed. "Are you crying?"

"No. No." Alice shook her head with too much vigor. Ever since she was a child. Alice had always acted this way whenever she was trying to keep tears from falling.

Vera set down her mending and moved toward her sister. "Alice, don't worry. I'll never leave you."

"Of course you will, you ninny! You'll leave the minute you marry." Alice gathered her handkerchief to her eyes.

"But I'll visit."

"Not from Baltimore, you won't. At least, not all that often." Alice sniffled.

"Oh, I'm sure you'll find someone else who'll be glad to take care of little Paul and the new baby once it arrives."

"It's more than that, and you know it. I won't be losing a nursemaid. I'll be losing my sister and best friend."

Vera rubbed her shoulder. "You won't ever lose me."

"Is that so? I hardly saw you when you were Mrs. Alden's companion in Baltimore, and now you've fallen in love with a man who promises to take you back there. Tell me, is city living all that special?"

Vera didn't have to think long before she answered. "It wasn't so special when I was a companion. Mind you, the Aldens made my life pleasant enough. You know, I hadn't thought much about this before you mentioned it, but now that I think of it, the idea of running my own house in the city—well, that would be tremendous indeed."

Alice's sniffles turned to sobs. "I wish I hadn't said anything. Now your ideas have grown larger than ever."

"Oh, Alice, can't you be happy for me?"

"I'd be happier if Byron Gates were a local farmer. Or a merchant in town."

"I know. And in some ways that would make me happier, too. If I do end up moving back to the city, I'll miss you. And little Paul." Vera brought her own lace handkerchief to her misty eyes. "Oh, I don't want to think about that. Aren't we both as silly as can be, daydreaming and planning a future that might not even happen?"

"Oh, it will happen if that's the Lord's will," Alice said. "And if Byron is the man who will make you happy and as long as he's a Christian, then I hope that marriage to him is what the Lord has in mind for you."

❧

Byron couldn't decide which made him more nervous—his experiences the night he dropped off the money, or the prospect of seeing Vera again. Just because he had gotten rid of the criminals didn't mean he was any more worthy of her now than he had been before, but at least he no longer had to fear for her safety now that the extortionists were in police custody. Was that good enough?

Lord, I don't deserve Vera, but I pray she will accept me all the same. I pray Thy will is to soften the hearts of her family, as well. In the name of Thy Son, amen.

Clarence had agreed to put him up during his stay and expected him to arrive at his home soon. But Byron was in no mood to face his friend—not until he had seen Vera. He couldn't wait to be near her again, to regard her lovely face, to inhale a breath of the light scent she wore, to be in the presence of her sweet warmth.

twenty-one

As Byron pulled up to Vera's drive, he took in a breath. Vera stood on the stoop, her posture relaxed. She was dressed in a lovely cream-colored frock. A pink ribbon accentuated her tiny waist. He watched her as the carriage approached. Suddenly her posture became charged with anticipation. Did she look forward to seeing him as much as he did her?

With the dignity of a lady, she stood in place and allowed him to greet her as he stepped onto the stoop.

"Byron, you're back earlier than I expected." Her eyes were wide with eagerness. "Do tell me what transpired in the city!"

"I have all the time in the world to tell you my story. At this moment, I only want to bask in the knowledge that we are together once more. If I may be so bold, I couldn't wait to return to you." In a sudden impulse, he took her petite hand in his and brushed his lips against the back of her knuckles.

She looked at him through softened eyes. "I see your charm has only increased since your stay in the city."

"As has your own." He made a show of observing her and smiled in approval. "Surely you didn't dress for me. You must be on your way to an engagement?"

"An ice-cream social at Lily's. Why, didn't Clarence tell you? I'm certain he was invited."

"I didn't stop by Clarence's yet. I wanted to see you first."

She averted her eyes. "I am honored."

"Clarence is a social fellow. No doubt if he's been invited to eat a bit of ice cream with friends, he didn't linger for me. I'll just be on my way so you can go to the social. By your leave, we can meet tomorrow, perhaps?"

"Never mind the social. They can all wait. Or better yet, you and I can stay here and feast on the peach ice cream I churned today for the event. They'll never miss me."

"Anyone in his right mind would miss you. I did while I was in Baltimore."

Her shy smile was his reward. "I have an idea. Why don't we both go to the ice-cream social, and then you can come back here with me, and we can sit for a spell."

"Are you sure Lily won't mind? And what about Alice? I don't want to do anything to antagonize her."

"Surely you jest. Everyone would be quite upset with me if I didn't bring you along to the social now that you're back. And as for Alice, well, I think maybe she has warmed up to you."

Byron couldn't imagine such a scenario, but he wanted to believe Vera. And the idea of seeing his friends in the country again appealed to him. Sharing good times at the social would prolong his time with Vera. All were good reasons to comply with her suggestion.

Alice stepped out onto the stoop.

"Good evening, Mrs. Sharpe."

"Good evening, Mr. Gates. I didn't expect you to be back so soon." Though she didn't look at him as though she were greeting a long-lost friend, Byron did sense a little less frigidity in her face and tone.

"My business in Baltimore is complete, Mrs. Sharpe. I hope you don't mind that I stopped by to see your sister."

"No, but she was just on her way out. Mr. Sharpe had planned to take her to see a friend." Alice turned toward the door and called, "Elmer! Did you get the ice cream?"

"Getting it now!" His voice sounded muffled.

Vera placed a hand on her sister's arm. "You don't mind if Byron takes me instead, do you? I know Elmer really doesn't want to go, and everyone will be ever so happy to see Byron again."

Alice didn't answer right away. Keeping her expression even, she answered, "I'm sure."

"I would be honored to escort Miss Vera to the social, with your permission, Mrs. Sharpe."

"Oh, please, Alice?"

Alice twisted her lips. "Vera! You needn't beg."

"Then it's quite all right. Good!" Vera smiled and kissed her sister on the cheek. "Thank you, Alice."

Byron sent Alice a grateful look. Her eyes were soft, her lips not set in a stern line. For once, he felt she might even like him. One day.

&

Despite being in Byron's company during the ice-cream social, Vera thought the event would never end. She was eager to learn everything that had transpired in Baltimore. At least she knew by his presence that he remained in one piece, and a lack of bruises on his face told her he hadn't engaged in fisticuffs. Those two facts kept her spirit fueled through the gathering.

As soon as they could excuse themselves from Lily's without seeming impolite, Vera nudged Byron in an unspoken plea for them to leave the party. He didn't hesitate to comply, and soon they found themselves back in the carriage.

"Here we are," Byron said with too much gusto when they pulled into the Sharpe farm drive.

"Yes." Vera trembled with anticipation. "Will you visit with me for a spell in the parlor? It's really not so late."

"I would be honored."

Under Alice's watchful and begrudging eye, Vera prepared

tea as Byron passed the time in easy conversation with Elmer, who didn't voice any objection when she took Byron into the parlor. Vera knew full well that Alice would be keeping an open ear. The thought didn't worry her as she escorted Byron into the parlor.

"I've been waiting to hear your news from Baltimore, Byron. Please, tell me what happened," Vera implored.

"You don't take any time for pleasantries before getting right to the point, do you?" Though his tone suggested playfulness, he shifted on his side of the mahogany divan.

"We've spoken in pleasantries all evening. Pleasantries I have hoped it was my right to enjoy. After all, you did wire me that the engagement with Miss Estes is officially broken. Is that still true?"

He nodded.

"I'm so sorry."

"Don't be. Daisy and I were childhood friends, and the match was one between our families rather than between us. Mr. Estes especially wanted the match because he envisioned our family businesses combining into a powerful enterprise."

"Romantic, isn't he?"

Byron chuckled. "In his own way, he wants what's best for his daughter."

"He reminds me of someone else I could mention." Vera looked pointedly toward the kitchen so Byron would know she referred to her sister.

"Yes. We are both blessed with families who love us, even if their visions for us are not always what we would have for ourselves."

An unhappy thought crossed her mind. "I hope all is well with the Estes family now."

"Yes. I think they all shall recover. Why, I even expect to see

Daisy's engagement announcement in the paper soon."

"Good." A relieved sigh escaped Vera's lips. "Then there is a happy ending for all concerned."

"Except for me. But that may change."

twenty-two

Suddenly the parlor seemed silent. Vera watched Byron shift in his seat. She clasped her hands, tensing.

"You. . .you think your life may change soon? How?" Vera suspected, but she wanted to hear the words.

"My happiness depends on your reaction to our conversation here tonight."

"You are placing quite a bit of responsibility on my shoulders."

"I ask you to take no responsibility that you find too burdensome. All I ask is that you be honest with me."

"I always have been, and I always will be."

"I'll start by reiterating that no one expects me to marry Daisy. No one."

"That's a blessing. I hope settling that matter wasn't too painful."

"It wasn't pleasant. I'll spare you the details about that. Now for the extortionists." Byron took in a breath. "I notified the police, and they offered their help. Apparently these men have been making sport—and a great deal of money—with false claims of debts owed by known gamblers. They assumed that men such as these would be unwilling to go to the police. And for a long time, they were proven right."

"But they didn't count on choosing an uncooperative target in you."

Byron smiled. "Indeed. True, I was a known gambler who wasted time and money—time and money I wish I could get back now, only that is impossible."

"I must confess, if I may be so bold, I don't understand the attraction of easy money, especially for a man such as yourself who is heir to a considerable fortune."

"That's a good question." Byron peered at the corner of the room for a moment, apparently immersed in thought. "One I haven't contemplated."

"You don't have to answer, then."

"No, I think I should, especially since you are a friendly audience. No doubt I will be asked that question repeatedly when I share my testimony, and I need to have a good answer." He pondered the idea only a few more seconds before responding. "I suppose any man, whether rich or poor, likes to feel that he has outwitted a worthy opponent. A gaming house, with the odds stacked in its favor, is a worthy opponent indeed. I remember the few times I did leave the halls with a good sum of money. I felt quite witty and that luck was on my side. Of course, now I know neither of these ideas held truth. When one plays games of chance often enough, one is bound to win sooner or later. And you can trust me, it is most often later."

"You mentioned that Clarence was gambling that night. Where were you?" Vera asked.

"I was watching him. He would return to me from time to time for more money."

"No doubt. But I must ask, weren't you tempted in the least to join him? I know Clarence well enough to surmise that he practically begged you to take part."

"As the saying goes, misery loves company." Byron chuckled. "I confess, I was a little apprehensive about going back to my old haunt. I thought I might be tempted. You don't think me too weak for that, I hope."

"No. I think it took courage for you to admit it to me. I am tempted, too."

"You? Why, I can't imagine a pure soul such as yours would find yourself in situations often where temptations abound."

"I do try to avoid occasions for sin." Vera didn't want to admit her weakness, but since Byron had taken such a bold stand and had spoken well about honesty, she knew she had to return the favor. "But of course, I'm far from perfect. I'll confess that I have been coveting a few yards of the most delicious cloth at the general store lately. It's a beautiful shade of red. Can you imagine? Red! And yet I'm so drawn to it that I find I cannot venture into the store without taking a peek at it. I often touch it, even. It's so soft I can't imagine I could sew anything practical out of it. And it costs much more than any decent person should spend on fabric. But my, it is beautiful." To her embarrassment, a sigh escaped her lips before she could stop it.

"That does sound beautiful. And I can understand why a woman as lovely as yourself would enjoy pretty fabric."

"True. Sadly, that does prove we all experience temptation in one form or another. How easily you seem to have overcome yours!"

"Only with God's aid. He helped me to see things I was unwilling to admit in the past: the desperation in some of the gamers' eyes and the look of the people who believed themselves to be having a good time but were, in fact, doing anything but."

"Funny how you can see things differently once you're looking at things from God's perspective. Of course, I have never set foot in a gaming hall, but I have seen people mired in sin. It's not a pretty sight. I rejoice that you have thrown off that yoke. Though in all probability you will face temptation again throughout your life, you have shown that you are able to resist it."

"And I am determined to resist temptation wherever it meets me from now on."

"But that doesn't answer the question as to what happened with the men."

"Oh yes. The police knew about these men and were more than happy to assist me in arresting them. I went to deliver the extortionists' money, knowing the police weren't far behind. As soon as Detective Pierce and his men gained enough evidence to assure conviction, they made themselves known to the criminals, and now I have no doubt they will be serving a good amount of time in prison."

"You'll be testifying in court?"

"I'm sure I will be called upon, yes."

"How exciting!"

"Living through such excitement is not as glamorous as one might think, although I suppose such adventure sounds enticing to a person who has never encountered the criminal element. The experience made me all the more grateful for what our police do for us every day. In this case, not only did they assure my safety, but with the capture of the criminals, they have ensured your safety and Daisy's, as well."

"My safety?"

He winced. "Yes. Once I assured them I was no longer associated with Daisy, they threatened you."

Vera gasped. "They had heard rumors about our relationship."

"Yes. That they would stop at nothing to find out anything they could about me and that they threatened people close to me made them especially dangerous."

"So you were right," Vera realized out loud. "They did plan to keep bleeding you for who knows how long."

"Until I was too poor to be of further interest to them," Byron said.

"This time I will beg your forgiveness, and you can't stop me. I truly regret giving you such terrible advice about how to handle the situation."

"Please, you were only sharing your opinion. I respect you more than any other woman I know except my own mother, but I would not look to you first and foremost as an expert on the average extortionist."

"I suppose not." She couldn't help but smile. "I'm glad you didn't listen to me and that you summoned the police. I was afraid the men would make good on their threats of violence upon you if you told the police."

"That's understandable. And I admit, I was nervous at first, too. But hindsight is always superior vision, and I'm glad I got the police involved. Your concern for my well-being gratifies me. I must say it was tough going for me during my conversation with the men. But that's over now, and all is resolved. Except for what that means for you and me."

She took in a breath. "What do you mean?"

"I'm saying that if I hadn't learned my lesson about returning to my past way of life when I took Clarence to the gaming hall, I certainly did after my encounter with the extortionists."

"This is all Clarence's fault. If he hadn't insisted on that bet, you never would have been in Baltimore that night, and they would have chosen some other man to bilk."

"And they would still be doing their vile business, ruining many men in the process. I believe God used this to work to the good. Not only did He show me again and again not to be tempted by gaming, but He used me to bring evil men to justice."

Vera pondered his words. "You have something there. I am always amazed by how the Lord works."

"I am becoming more amazed by Him myself, every day."

"Now if the Lord can only reform Clarence."

Byron chuckled. "Clarence's heart never has been as hard as mine was. If God can change me, He can change Clarence. I have a feeling He will." He paused. "So what about you, Vera? Do you think you could sustain interest in a man with a checkered past?"

Her heart beat faster. This was the moment for which she had been waiting, yet the idea of committing boldly left her feeling shy. "I hope you don't mean Clarence."

"No, I don't." His eyes held a hopeful light. "I mean, now that I have discarded my past and have no interest in returning to it and now that your safety is assured, I hope you will allow me to ask Elmer if I might court you in earnest."

"Yes. Yes. I would like that." Her voice sounded much smaller than she desired. "Why don't you ask him now?" As soon as she made the suggestion, she regretted sounding so forward.

"That is the most splendid idea I've heard all evening. I'd like to talk to him now." He rose from his seat.

Moments later, Vera wasted no time in running to Alice in the kitchen while the men retreated into Elmer's study.

Alice sat at the table, relaxing after putting Paul to bed. "Is Byron asking Elmer what I think he's asking?"

"Yes, and you are not going to do a thing to stop it. I've never been happier."

"I know. I can see it in your eyes. And no, I won't object if Elmer agrees. I've been selfish long enough. It's time for me to let you go so you can find your own happiness. You have served others long, well, and sweetly, Vera. You deserve love with Byron if that is where you have found it."

"I have."

"Then I see no reason why Elmer won't give his consent."

Moments later, both men emerged from the library. Vera

could see from Byron's relieved and happy expression that all had gone well.

"Come, let us enjoy the stars," Vera said.

Alice raised her eyebrows, but Vera chose to ignore her. Her turn had finally arrived, and she was not planning to let any admonishment mar the moment.

She didn't wait long after the door shut behind them to speak. "Well, what happened?"

Byron broke into a smile. "He gave me his permission. Now my only hopes are that you don't mind the prospect of moving back to Baltimore and that you don't want an exceedingly long courtship."

"No, I don't mind the prospect of moving back to Baltimore, even though I'll miss everyone here terribly. And no, I don't want an exceedingly long courtship."

"Good. That's what I was hoping you would say."

She looked deeply into his eyes. Studying them with such intensity, she almost didn't realize that his lips approached hers until they met her mouth. They felt softer than she expected and even warmer than she had imagined. The tenderness yet strength of his embrace assured her that she would always be loved.

epilogue

October 1904

Byron clasped Vera's hand in his and led Vera to an alcove outside the little white church. The leaves on the trees nearby had begun to turn, providing a glorious backdrop for the day.

"Byron, what are you doing, making me leave our own wedding reception? Don't you know they'll miss us?"

Looking even more dashing than usual in his finely tailored wedding suit, he held her hands in his. "True. You are conspicuously lovely today. Not that today is any different from any other in that regard. You are so beautiful I must kiss you right this moment."

Byron made good on his promise. His warm embrace made the brisk autumn day seem as though a lovely summer sun shone. Her heart increased its beating as their lips met, emotions taking Vera to a world where she didn't care about the reception or even the prospect of a honeymoon in Europe. All she cared about was that she was finally Mrs. Byron Gates.

A cheerful female voice, now familiar to Vera, interrupted. "There you are, you two lovebirds."

Reluctantly they broke their kiss.

"Mother," Byron greeted her. "You're not asking us to go back to the reception yet, are you?"

"Clearly you have forgotten your manners, leaving your guests to their own devices," the elder Mrs. Gates, looking attractive herself in blue, said. "Although I must say there is no lack of food and good music. Your sister outdid herself in planning your wedding, Vera."

"Yes, she did." Vera thought perhaps she was the only person in the world who appreciated just how much her sister's efforts meant. She looked to Byron for confirmation and noticed that he was peering off in another direction. "What do you see that's so fascinating, Byron?"

Byron didn't miss a beat. "That blond man. I—I've seen him before. The night. . ."

"The night?" Mrs. Gates prodded.

Byron cleared his throat. "The night I made the payment to my kidnappers. He interrupted us, and they panicked. Because of him, I got a reprieve."

"What?" Vera asked. "Mr. Ginson was there? What was he doing in Baltimore?"

"You know him?" Surprise was evident in Byron's voice.

"Yes, he's a friend of Elmer's." Immediately seeing what must have happened, Vera exclaimed, "Byron! Do you suppose Elmer sent Mr. Ginson to Baltimore to help you?"

"I—I don't know. Would he do that for me?" Byron nearly choked with emotion.

"Yes," Mrs. Gates said. "I recall you mentioning a blond man. If you know him, Vera, then your brother-in-law must have interceded to help you both."

"I—I'll have to thank Elmer," Byron said. "And his friend. Although there's nothing I can do to repay them."

"You can repay them with your happiness," Mrs. Gates advised.

"That will be easy enough," Byron agreed and gazed into Vera's eyes. Unabashed now that they were married, Vera returned his look of love.

"Well," said Mrs. Gates, "I did have a reason for chasing you two out here. I wanted to see you alone before you left for the honeymoon. I have something for you, Vera."

"For me?" Vera felt a catch in her throat. She knew that Mrs. Gates had once wanted Byron to marry Daisy Estes. But during Vera's courtship with Byron, she and the older woman had discovered a mutual love of books, leading to intriguing discussions. Soon Vera had developed a genuine fondness for her future mother-in-law, a fact Vera knew pleased Byron. "You didn't need to give me a special gift, Mrs. Gates."

"Oh, but I want to. Very much." Her face looked soft; her eyes, so much like Byron's. "You have made my son very happy. I want to thank you for that." She handed Vera a black velvet box. "Look inside."

Vera opened the gift and gasped. "Pearls!"

"Yes. Those pearls were given to me by Byron's mother the day we married. I wore them on my honeymoon." Her voice sounded dreamy. "I had them restrung for you, and I hope you will enjoy them for many years."

Vera took in a breath. "They're beautiful. I would be honored to wear them. Your gesture means more than I can express. Thank you!"

The women embraced, with Byron observing.

"I think those pearls will look especially nice with that beautiful red dress Byron ordered for you," Mrs. Gates opined.

"Mother!" Byron chastised her.

Her eyes widened. "I'm sorry. Did I say something wrong?"

Byron sent his mother an indulgent look. "That's all right. I was going to surprise Vera, but the secret's out now."

"What?" Vera pressed.

"Remember telling me about the red fabric you coveted in the store? I bought it, and Alice made me a lovely gown for you, using a pattern from the latest Paris fashion."

Vera couldn't speak for a moment. "I don't know what makes me happier—that you did such a wonderful thing for me or that Alice and you worked together on such a sweet gift." She felt her eyes mist. "You truly have made this the most exquisite day of my life."

"That's what I wanted to hear," Byron said. "And you, too, Mother." Byron then hugged his mother. "Thank you for giving Vera the pearls. I think Grandmother would be thrilled."

"As do I." Mrs. Gates latched the strand around Vera's neck.

"How do they look?" Vera modeled the pearls.

"Lovely," Byron and Mrs. Gates agreed.

Mrs. Gates clasped Vera's hand and let it go. "I'll see you two back at the reception. Don't tarry too long. This day is brief, and you have your whole honeymoon ahead of you."

"Indeed," Byron told Vera as his mother disappeared, "our future is before us."

"Yes. And we shall live happily ever after," Vera murmured as she and her new husband melted into another kiss.

A Letter To Our Readers

Dear Reader:

In order that we might better contribute to your reading enjoyment, we would appreciate your taking a few minutes to respond to the following questions. We welcome your comments and read each form and letter we receive. When completed, please return to the following:

Fiction Editor
Heartsong Presents
PO Box 719
Uhrichsville, Ohio 44683

1. Did you enjoy reading *Vera's Turn for Love* by Tamela Hancock Murray?
   ❏ Very much! I would like to see more books by this author!
   ❏ Moderately. I would have enjoyed it more if

   _____
   _____
   _____

2. Are you a member of **Heartsong Presents**? ❏ Yes ❏ No
   If no, where did you purchase this book? _____
   _____

3. How would you rate, on a scale from 1 (poor) to 5 (superior), the cover design? _____

4. On a scale from 1 (poor) to 10 (superior), please rate the following elements.

   ____ Heroine   ____ Plot
   ____ Hero   ____ Inspirational theme
   ____ Setting   ____ Secondary characters

5. These characters were special because? _____

_____

_____

6. How has this book inspired your life? _____

_____

_____

7. What settings would you like to see covered in future
   Heartsong Presents books? _____

_____

_____

8. What are some inspirational themes you would like to see
   treated in future books? _____

_____

_____

9. Would you be interested in reading other **Heartsong
   Presents** titles? ☐ Yes ☐ No

10. Please check your age range:
   ☐ Under 18   ☐ 18-24
   ☐ 25-34   ☐ 35-45
   ☐ 46-55   ☐ Over 55

Name _____

Occupation _____

Address _____

City, State, Zip_____

Hearts♥ng

Any 12
Heartsong
Presents titles
for only
$27.00*

HISTORICAL ROMANCE IS CHEAPER BY THE DOZEN!

Buy any assortment of twelve *Heartsong Presents* titles and save 25% off of the already discounted price of $2.97 each!

*plus $2.00 shipping and handling per order and sales tax where applicable.

HEARTSONG PRESENTS TITLES AVAILABLE NOW:

(If ordering from this page, please remember to include it with the order form.)

Presents

Great Inspirational Romance at a Great Price!

Heartsong Presents books are inspirational romances in contemporary and historical settings, designed to give you an enjoyable, spirit-lifting reading experience. You can choose wonderfully written titles from some of today's best authors like Peggy Darty, Sally Laity, DiAnn Mills, Colleen L. Reece, Debra White Smith, and many others.

When ordering quantities less than twelve, above titles are $2.97 each.
Not all titles may be available at time of order.